Son of resident missionaries, **Barrie Sherwood** was born in Hong Kong in 1971. After moving to Canada he read English at Simon Fraser, British Columbia, and Concordia. He currently lives in Vancouver with his wife and daughter.

Leonard Walker was Professor of Archaeology at Nara Junior Women's College and Associate Advisor of the Nara National Cultural Properties Research Institute of the Agency for Cultural Affairs. He devoted thirteen years to excavating the site of the ancient palace of Nara and authored many insightful essays on his findings, including "Polyethylene Glycol and Freeze-Drying Techniques for Wooden Artefacts" (1981), "A Mocha Migration" (1981), and "Ancient Disposal: Rice Paddy Septic Fields" (1983), which won the Toyo Bunko Nihon Prize for outstanding contribution to national cultural studies. Late in 1994, Walker's wife, Marilyn, returned to the United States and filed for divorce. The emotional toll upon Walker was heavy. Soon after, he left home and career to take up residence among the 2000 secluded islands of the Philippines. It was from the idyllic isle of Boracay that he first made contact with Marcos Press of Manila to arrange for the publication of *The Pillow Book of Lady Kasa*. Mr. Walker's last correspondence with Marcos Press came in March of 1996; it consisted of his introduction to the text, the final money-order, and a written request that the first copy be sent to his wife.

Lady Kasa was born 12 centuries ago (?720) and served as Lady-in-Waiting to the Princess Takano during the middle years of the Nara Period. It is unknown if she was ever married, but she was in love, for a time, with the illustrious Otomo Yakamochi, then Governor of Etchu Province. Twenty-nine tanka professing her love, devotion, and, later, contempt for Yakamochi, have been preserved in the *Collection of 10,000 Leaves* ('*Manyoshu*') the great anthology of Naran poetry. Early in 747, Kasa left Nara. Her life after her Court service came to an end is totally obscure.

BARRIE SHERWOOD

The Pillow Book
of Lady Kasa

To Anne Hungerford,
For "Directed Studies"

LIVRES
DC
BOOKS

CONTENTS

INTRODUCTION
by Leonard Walker

THE PILLOW BOOK OF LADY KASA

DC New Writers Series edited by Robert Allen

Cover design by Gerald Luxton
Typesetting in **Gadget** and Georgia by Andy Brown

An excerpt from the text was previously published in Matrix Magazine, Number 53.

Printed in Canada

Canadian Cataloguing in Publication Data

Sherwood, Barrie 1971-
    The Pillow Book of Lady Kasa

ISBN 0-919688-68-3 (bound) - ISBN 0-919688-66-7 (pbk.)

1. Title

PS8587.H389P54 2000   C813'.6   C00-900834-9
PR9199.3.S5128P54 2000

DC Books
950 rue Décarie, Montreal, Quebec, Canada, H4L 4V9

DC Books acknowledges the support of the Canada Council for the Arts and of Sodec for our publishing program.

THE CANADA COUNCIL | LE CONSEIL DES ARTS
FOR THE ARTS | DU CANADA
SINCE 1957 | DEPUIS 1957

To Patricia

and for Jean and Red

INTRODUCTION

Makura no soshi ('notes of the pillow') was a generic term for an informal book of notes which men and women of old Japan composed when they retired to their rooms in the evening. In modern days the genre has picked up unseemly connotations, but in truth there was never anything inherently licentious about pillow books; the name simply derives from the fact that they were often kept inside pillows. The pillow used by the Naran aristocracy, it should be pointed out, was more obstinate a bed companion than the downy sack of today; it was a heavy wooden box, ten inches in height, that featured a hard, flat, brocaded surface on top, and shallow inset drawers where may have been found combs, bits of jewellery, a perfume ball or — *le voilà* — one's notebook.

Long the only *makura no soshi* thought to have survived to the present day is that of Sei Shonagon, a lady-in-waiting at the court of the Empress Sadako during the Heian Period (794–1185). It is a vast and discursive miscellany of anecdotes, poems, character sketches, and highly subjective lists of good and bad, pretty and ugly, funny and pitiful, admirable and tasteless. It provides such a detailed picture of contemporary court life that Mr. Arthur Waley has called it "the most important document of the period that we possess."[1] The redoubtable Mr. Ivan Morris has added that, although Sei Shonagon's pillow book is the only one of its type known to have survived from ancient Japan, "It is possible that many others were written."[2] Keeping this statement in mind, it would seem less doubtful to certain critical orientalists that

---

[1] Waley, Arthur, *The Pillow Book of Sei Shonagon*, George Allen and Unwin Ltd., London, 1979, p. 14.

[2] Morris, Ivan, *The Pillow Book of Sei Shonagon*, Columbia University Press, New York, 1967, p. 11.

another pillow book has recently come to light: *The Pillow Book of Lady Kasa*.

The value of an artefact is highly (but not entirely) contingent upon the age to which it belongs. According to the Agency for Cultural Affairs, there are three classifications for archaeological 'finds'. Generally speaking, any artefact belonging to pre-Showa Period (1926-1989) society is classified a 'Significant Find'; any artefact from the Edo Period (1603-1868) is classified a 'Major Find'; and artefacts which shed light on pre-Edo culture are 'National Treasures'. For the dancing, radiant beam it casts into the mists of the remote Nara Period (710-794), *The Pillow Book of Lady Kasa* surely exceeds any such classification. It is one of the great archaeological discoveries of Japanese history. Before going on to examine the pillow book, however, it is well to learn some more about the halcyon age of Japanese civilisation.

History, in fact, begins with the Nara Period.

In pre-history and proto-history, economic and political power in Japan had been centred on the north coast of the island of Kyushu, where proximity to Korea allowed for interaction with the continent's powerful culture. But because hot, swampy, volcano-studded Kyushu had little advantage apart from its geographical location, once it was consolidated, political power tended to gravitate eastward to richer land and a more central location on the island of Honshu. About AD 350 a great expedition made its way from Kyushu along the northern shore of the Inland Sea. Despite stubborn resistance from Neolithic Ainu locals, they eventually landed at Naniwa, at the mouth of the Yodogawa river. It was not far from here, in the fertile Yamato Basin to the east, that Japanese culture began to flourish.

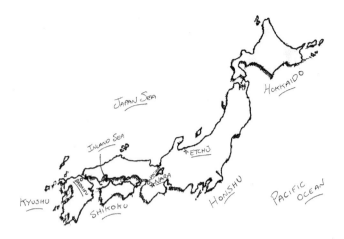

1. The Japanese Archipelago

At the expedition's arrival, the Emperor Jimmu Tenno was enthroned beside the Yodogawa river at Kashiwabara. The specific site is now occupied by the 7-Eleven Store near Yodoya Bashi Station, on the Mido-suji Line. Needless to point out then, the capital did not remain here. According to an ancient belief that a dwelling place was polluted by death, it was customary upon the demise of a sovereign for his successor to move into a new palace. Thus, for the following four centuries, the centre of government was repeatedly shifted around Yamato and the neighbouring provinces.

In terms of practicality this superstition is ridiculous. On an emotional level, however, it is not beyond our understanding. Consider Lady Gemmyo, whose son was the Emperor Mommu: In spring of 709, young Mommu returned to the Fujiwara capital from a visit to the cherry orchards at Yoshino. On arrival he complained of headaches and nausea more severe than those usually brought about by mere saké. Doctors, priests, and diviners, summoned to his bedside,

3

made efforts to revive the ailing young man, but in the forenoon of the next day he passed away. Lady Gemmyo had no choice but to attend the complex funereal ceremonies that followed, the tedium of which she must have found all but unbearable. Is it any wonder she left the capital's silent halls and flagrantly empty gardens behind?

Thus, in the year 710, Gemmyo acceded to the throne and moved the capital to Heijo, or as it came to be known, Nara.[3] The specific location was chosen because it met perfectly the requirements of Chinese geomancy which was then, like most things Chinese, in high esteem. The directional code of the 'Four Birds and Beasts' — cyan dragon, scarlet phoenix, white tiger, and dusky warrior — stipulated the need for a river to the east, a low and damp area to the south, a long road to the west, and a rise to the north. Moreover, practices of divination by interpreting melons (pepomancy) and cracks in burnt tortoise shells (plastromancy) had pinpointed Nara as an ideal location for commerce and industry. Doubtless, such augury is nonsense to the present reader, but it was proven valid in the minds of the ancients when, in 741, Emperor Shomu moved the capital away from Nara. The gods chafed violently at their desertion: Shomu's efforts to build a new capital met with failure, and the country was rocked with earthquakes day and night. On the advice of Nara's priests and diviners he soon returned to Nara, and the gods were appeased.

Aside from being geomantically propitious, Nara was practical, a diminutive model of the great Chinese capital of Chang'an. The bilateral, gridiron layout of the city streets was entered from the south, along Scarlet Phoenix Boulevard

---

3 Nara: Two simple syllables, so richly endowed. There is no meaning universally agreed upon by scholars, but the word, at least, has a regal posture in lieu of a definition. I have always envisioned the N as an heraldic bend on the white escutcheon of the page. Or the lapel of an Empress's robe. Or, better, the king's bandoleer — a's in obeisance, r the defiant prince.

(alternately translated, by those of no poetic ability, as 'Red Finch Road' and 'Vermilion Sparrow Avenue'.) A capacious seventy-five metres wide and lined with willows and orange trees, this magnificent thoroughfare bisected the city and ran for nearly four kilometres, past houses progressively larger and more elaborate, to Scarlet Phoenix Gate at its northern end. This in turn was the main south entrance to the Imperial Palace, a city in itself.

By far the most developed Japanese city of its time, Nara boasted over fifty Buddhist temples and Shinto shrines, a Confucian university, the expansive and elegant halls of the Imperial Palace Compound, two markets – one on each side of Scarlet Phoenix Boulevard – that were open on alternating weeks, and at least a dozen private and state-owned saké breweries. An early form of money economy was beginning to prevail and trade was steadily expanding. The population, at its height, reached 200,000. In a valley of rice paddies, bamboo forests, and crude pit-houses, the metropolis of Nara — its streets laid out in a rigorous grid, its gardens sculptured in the latest Chinese style, its 'skyline' bristling with pagodas — stood out as a paradise of safety, prosperity, and order. (Of course, time has reversed what the Narans wrought. All that remains of Nara Palace today is a swath of rice land and swamp, cherry trees, a lonely museum, the tracks of the Kintetsu Line, and a dusty soccer pitch I used to frequent after work, while revolving all around it are the truck tires, restaurants, and department-store doors of the burgeoning city that is its namesake.)

The Naran aristocracy were a sensitive people, appreciative of beauty, and in that respect their capital had no peer. In song and dance and, above all, poetry, they poured out their proud exuberance. The pre-eminent poetry collection of the period, the *Collection of 10,000 Leaves* ('*Manyoshu*'), contains no shortage of praise:

> The Imperial city of fairest Nara
> glows now at the height of beauty
> like brilliant flowers in bloom!

Down the middle of a wide boulevard parades a youthful gallant wearing robes of clashing hues and a silver-wrought sword. A lady of the Court, unrestricted as yet by the mean mores of medieval society, strolls along by herself in the shade, trailing her multi-coloured skirts. They meet at a bridge over the Sahogawa river and continue together, making enjoyable conversation beneath the zelkova trees. It is this picture of the gay metropolis which the exile to a foreign land, or the soldier stationed at one of the empire's lonely outposts, can never forget, and which causes him the most unbearable pangs of nostalgia. His is an Odyssean pain of separation:

> Although across the plains of the sea I have come
> passing through two thousand islands,
> not once has the city of Nara
> left my heart.

Unlike subsequent anthologies filled with jejune compositions by the bepowdered poetasters and pampered minions of the Heian Court, the *Collection of 10,000 Leaves* is typified by a genuineness of feeling. In his *An Anthology of Japanese Literature* (Grove Press, 1955), Mr. Donald Keene has praised it accordingly as "one of the world's great collections of poetry." Compiled in its final form in the eighth century, in good part by Lady Kasa's lover, Otomo Yakamochi, the anthology contains 4516 poems arranged in twenty volumes. Embodying strength of feeling, sincerity, and simplicity, these poems are the purest expression of the Naran spirit, untainted as yet by the perversions of the *samurai*. Whole sections of the collection deal with the recurring themes of love's sensuality and spirituality, and, especially, the sorrow of separation:

> Had I but known the way love left the world
> I would have built a barrier,
> between our dying love and death.[4]

Unfortunately, even as the *Collection of 10,000 Leaves* was being finished, a vogue for Chinese prose and poetry was taking possession of court circles. It lasted for over one hundred years, from the late Nara Period to the early Heian, and the result was gross neglect of Japanese literature. Only with the appearance of the great Murasaki Shikibu (*The Tale of Genji*) and Sei Shonagon (*The Pillow Book of Sei Shonagon*) did native literature regain at least a measure of the respect it had commanded in the Nara Period.

Apart from practicality and the formal beauty praised in its poetry, Buddhism was Nara's greatest strength, a factor not to be overlooked in comprehending the city's longevity. Buddhism had been introduced from Korea several centuries earlier, and had found a strong following alongside the native Shinto religion. Nara became the site of the greatest and most powerful Buddhist temples; by the middle of the century there were no fewer than forty-eight Buddhist temples within its precincts. In Naran society, consequently,

---

[4] Unless otherwise noted, all excerpted poetry comes from: De Bary, Theodore, Ed., *Collection of 10,000 Leaves,* Columbia University Press, New York, 1965.

Buddhism ascended to an unheralded level of importance, the state and church entwined to a degree equalled in the west only by the Vatican. As one can see from a short look at the *Collection of 10,000 Leaves,* traditionally Buddhist sentiments concerning life's vanity and evanescence such as 'life is frail' (one might well substitute 'love' in this case) and 'nothing endures' soon added a melancholy note to the hitherto charmed province of Japanese poetry:

> How I loathe the twin seas
> of being and non being
> and yearn for the island
> of bliss, untouched by
> the changing tides.

At the start of the eighth century the Buddhist clergy were the prepotent force in Japanese politics, but more and more they faced tenacious and inventive opposition from the Fujiwara, a large and influential family of the highest social standing. Surprisingly, the Fujiwara never commanded any significant military strength, physical force being the least important of their methods of persuasion and assimilation. Instead, this aristocratic and influential clan forged infrangible links between themselves and the imperial family through 'marriage politics': the wedding of Fujiwara daughters to reigning Emperors. By the late 700's the Fujiwara family had assimilated itself into the highest tiers of government. Marriage politics had pushed the clergy away from the centre of control, and the family was well on its way to establishing a predominance in national affairs which would last for centuries.

If you visit the city of Nara today, it is not difficult to understand why the ancients — secular and religious — were so much in love with it. Nineties Nara has not lost all of its old perfume. Walking through Nara Park, climbing into the pristine hills of the Eastern Nara Basin, twelve centuries are stripped away. The blinding pandemonium of *pachinko* parlours, the cataracts of shoppers in the covered streets, the megapolis of Osaka on the other side of Mount Ikoma, are all very far away from us. We follow the time-polished stones of an ancient road. Around us, we hear the bellowing of stags and the "ho-to-to! ho-to-to!" of the *hototoguisu*.[5] The only traffic likely to be encountered in these ancient, indifferent hills are elderly hikers passing by, all smiles and *"ohayo"*s and *"kawai desu-ne!"*s[6] in their over-engineered boots and genuine *lederhosen*. The following poem is not, one hopes, incongruous with the spirit of the rest for being penned twelve centuries later:

> Harmony on the autumn wind
> is the bell of Kofuku-ji.
> But the young bough
> rejects its burden of early snow.

It should be restated — right now — that Nara *was* the Golden Age. There was caprice on one hand and ignorance on the other, but there was no turmoil hidden behind the 'façade' of a happy relationship; nor decadence, nor even intrigue; no dirt for far-reaching and autopsical relatives to smear over its curtain of white brocade. Nara was as far removed from the age which spawned *haiku* and *Kabuki* and the tea ceremony as that age is from our own, but if it had few pretty contributions to make to popular culture in comparison with the Momoyama or Edo Periods, it had no *samurai* ('rednecks') either, no *shogun* ('tyrants'), no mercurial and

---

[5] *Cuculus poliocephalus*
[6] "Good morning" and "It's so pretty!"

9

merciless *ninja* ('assassins'), no *geisha* ('a prostitute is a prostitute'), no *seppuku* ('suicide'). The Narans peacefully, respectfully, at times happily, coexisted. What more could be expected of us, after all? The downfall, the licentious mess, only came in its wake.... As George Sansom stated in *A History of Japan to 1334*: "A distinguishing feature of the history of the following periods is the decay of institutions perpetuated from the Nara Period."

> Now that with the change of times
> Nara is become
> an Imperial City that was,
> the grass grows rank in the streets.

The grievous weakening of Imperial authority from the late Nara Period to the end of the Heian, due in part to the attrition of the Fujiwara clan, opened wide the gate for the rise of the military class. This led to the formation of feudalism which, for some seven centuries, totally changed the face of Japan. From the first ascendancy of this military system down to our own confused days, everything in society — ambition, honour, the very temperament of a man and his daily pursuits — has become thoroughly unlike that of which our authoress was an eye-witness. To this day, Japan has not yet recovered any more than a semblance of this ancient civilisation which it once attained and then lost.

Perhaps the pithiest expression of nostalgia for this ideal of the Nara Period is the word *sayonara*. Incorporated within its four lyrical syllables, you will note, is the name of that great city. Resounding a billion times a day, all across Honshu and Kyushu, Shikoku and Hokkaido and Okinawa, in Hawaii, in Guam, in São Paulo, in Vancouver, and even, perhaps, in Cape Cod, Massachusetts, *sayonara* is synonymous with yearning, a thinly veiled tribute to the halcyon days.

Until the appearance of *The Pillow Book of Lady Kasa*, our knowledge of Nara had been gathered from the *Collection of 10,000 Leaves*, early court histories, the considerable collection of art, fabric, scrolls, and musical instruments amassed by Emperor Shomu and preserved today in Nara's *Shoso-in* Museum (well worth a visit if you are in Nara), and, most importantly, archaeological excavations at the Nara Palace Site. The excavation of architectural ruins can tell us what an ancient city looked like, but without props the set remains barren. Cleeks and ladles and zithers and braziers enrich our understanding of people's everyday lives – their intimate concerns and daily routines – far more than any quadrangle of staid pillars. At Nara, one prop has been crucial: the humble *mokkan*.

Mokkan are narrow wooden tablets that were used by the Naran bureaucracy as order forms, receipts, time-cards, identification cards, cargo-tags, memos, and inventories. They were stamped and inscribed and tallied and snapped in two, hung from one's belt, hung from a peg, tied to a basket of crabs, strapped to a barrel of salt…. Most of those excavated from the Nara Palace Site were found at a depth of about one metre. Here they lay – safe from the plough and other disturbances – for over a thousand years, immersed in an airtight environment which protected them from the invasion of decay-causing bacteria. When, however, wood is waterlogged for such long periods, cellulose and the other resinous components of the wood are gradually leached away and their place is taken by the surrounding water. The wooden object, recently exhumed, may look structurally healthy, but as rapid desiccation ensues it is almost certain to shrink, crack, and crumble. There are three weapons available to the conserva-

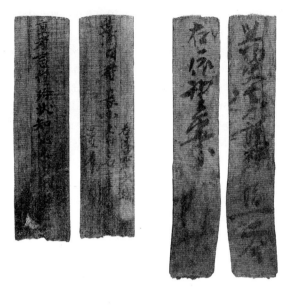

2. mokkan

tor to halt the deterioration of waterlogged *mokkan*: freeze-drying, PEG, and alcohol-ether-dammar.

For my entire career, I used the PEG method (my "never-ending affair with Peg", as my wife put it). Careful freeze-drying can provide some spectacular results, but I found that PEG, on the whole, was more reliable. (I never used the alcohol-ether-dammar method.)

PEG is an abbreviation for polyethylene glycol, a clear, odourless high polymer. For conserving waterlogged arte-facts, a 20 percent solution of PEG is maintained in a tank at a constant of 60 degrees Celsius and the artefacts are imme-diately plunged into it. Over time, as the water contained in the artefact begins to merge with the PEG solution, the con-centration of PEG in the tank is gradually increased until at last it stands at 98 to 100 per cent. The water originally trapped in the artefact will eventually be totally replaced by PEG. When the object is removed (the average *mokkan* needs a good six-month soak) and exposed to normal temperatures, the PEG hardens in place and the shape of the object is safely preserved.

In thirteen years, I myself oversaw the conservation of some 30,000 *mokkan*. Although no one can deny their early contribution to Nara studies, these ubiquitous sticks have become in recent years a source of mostly useless information. One typical *mokkan*, for instance, records the rather otiose fact that Mr. O-no Kasumaro, lower junior eighteenth rank, carpenter at the Ministry of Construction, did not show up for work on the 10th of April, 746. Why not, one may ask? Did he sleep in? Was he hit by an ox-cart? Gored by a boar? The tight-fisted earth reveals nothing else about Mr. Kasumaro. Other *mokkan* kindly inform us that the residence of Statesman Moroé ordered one *to* of red beans, fifteen *to* of oranges, and some pears from the Great Catering Office at an unknown date; taxes received from the province of Etchu in 747 came in the form of twenty *to* of dried shark meat; the Nara Palace Saké Bureau was destroyed one January; the Princess Takano's domicile was re-floored in 746, etcetera, etcetera, *ad infinitum*, all devoid of why and wherefore. For those who have spent their careers modelling forests with these woodchips, it is only too obvious the gap that *The Pillow Book of Lady Kasa* so elegantly (so effortlessly!) steps into.

How does the past fill a hole in the present? It never does, not sufficiently anyway. And I have an idea that with our shoddy eyes we perceive holes in our knowledge and our lives, and set about to fill them with pieces of the past. But nothing comes from the ground, or from the ocean, or from an attic or a well or a tomb that was not already in the air. Could we sharpen our perceptions, I believe we could leave off digging. A preposterous claim? I am perhaps the last person in the world who could prove it. So I continue on with the tale of the pillow book's discovery:

In spring of 1995, a proverbially aged widow, cleaning out her proverbially fecund attic, slipped from the ladder, smacked her head on a rung and died. When the family descended upon the house to despoil and dispose of old Ms. Ogawa's things, hidden among the more obvious treasure and patent junk were several cloth-bound books written in an almost illegible script. Luckily, there was one sensitive member of the Ogawa clan present to save them from the *gomi* pile. Ms. Nami Ogawa, with perspicacity I myself had cultivated in several college courses, recognized their value and wasted no time contacting my office.

As I recall, I was poring over the floor-plan of Sogo Family Department Store the day she called. I had been kept from the dig by heavy rains and was trying to determine under which sordid department — lingerie, patisserie, wines of Bordeaux, or the Via Appia Boutique — lay the remains of drainage ditch SK 414, a particularly rich source of *mokkan* that I had spent the previous month tracking and excavating across the Sogo parking lot. The task had not been easy; I had been exposed to much vented ire from drivers intent on utilizing the asphalt I was in the process of removing. Why was I wrecking the parking lot? they would inevitably ask. Was I looking for treasure?

No, a ditch.

A *ditch?* You're digging a ditch to find a ditch?

Any explanations I offered only seemed to compound frustrations. It was not long before I resorted to the use of a large sign warning of biological hazard. The Japanese can be very fastidious about hygiene; the spectacle of a red-haired foreigner in orange rubber, working beneath the logo of a grimacing purple virus frightened their sensibilities enough to afford me a modicum of peace. At least until the fire department arrived, but this becomes peripheral.

In my memory the office is very bright when Ms. Ogawa calls. The afternoon sun beams directly through the window, shining on the surface of the desk and making a resplendent map of the rather dull floor-plan spread before me. The telephone, when it rings, sounds like Balinese wind-chimes. Unfortunately, memory also tells me that I had long since disconnected the buzzer in my telephone, my window faced north, in the shadow of the western gym, and the rain had been thrumming against the glass all morning. The reality is, I felt no premonition whatsoever when I saw the little red square blinking on Line 1. Ms. Ogawa's voice was one of those 'sensei voices', all politeness and squeaky rectitude until kneaded with a little humour:

"Ms. Ogawa, what did the archaeologist say to his unruly son? Hei-jo! Stop mokkan around!... Well?"

"Can I see you?" she asked.

"Of course," I replied. "My door is always open to a partner-in-learning."

"Thank-you, sensei, but can you come to my home? It is at Ikoma Mountain. Hosan-ji Station."

Now I was an exemplary mentor but I had yet to start making house calls. "Yes, I know the station, Ms. Ogawa. And certainly, were it not for the storm, I might consider coming. But the roads may be flooded today. You understand."

A moment of muffled silence. Then she asked, quite sincerely: "Don't you have a Land Rover?"

"Ms. Ogawa," I replied patiently, "I am not a big game

hunter. I do not go on safari as a rule."

She suggested the train.

A fine suggestion indeed, but I still did not know why I was going.

"Because," she said, "I've found something."

"What kind of something?" playing the game.

"Something *old*," she replied. And then, just as casually as if she were saying "strawberry" or "panda bear", she said: "A pillow book."

The idea was worthy not of skepticism but of outright dismissal. Still, one must nurture a curiosity. "Are you quite sure?" I answered. "Pillow books are a rather rare commodity."

"I found it in my nanna's attic."

"A pillow book."

"Yes."

"I see…. Well, that is very good indeed."

She must have read the tone of my voice for she countered immediately: "*Sensei*, people in Europe find Van Goghs in their garages all the time!"

"Yes, yes, Ms. Ogawa, they do or at least have done, certainly, one supposes, at least. Very well then, let's put your dating skills to work."

"*Really?*"

"Can you guess what period it's from?"

"Oh," she said disappointedly, "well, it's very old. Maybe… Nara Period…?"

From Nara the Kintetsu Line train courses across the fields of the Nara Palace Site towards Saidai-ji Station, hub and hubbub of suburban shopping malls and trains heading up and down the Nara Valley. If one continues west, in the direction of Osaka, the peak of Mount Ikoma looms progressively closer, dodging from one window of the train to the other, until it is finally cornered at Ikoma City.

From Ikoma, one has three options to reach Hosan-ji: *takushi* (the meter starts at ¥650); 3000 skewered, ankle-hungry stone steps; or the pre-war funicular which jingles up the slope to the tune of a paltry ¥230. Another 2000, 5000, or 230, respectively, will take you to the very top of Mount Ikoma for fabulous views over the Nara Valley on one side and Osaka, known as Naniwa during the Nara Period, on the other. Unfortunately, any tranquillity one might have hoped for on a mountain peak is completely obliterated by the Zippers, Whirly-gigs, Ninjas and Teacups of Ikoma Skyland Amusement Park.

Ding! Ding! The choice is dear. The wooden benches creak. The doors wheeze shut. The old lady sitting next to you with a plastic bag of crabs in her lap coughs and apologizes. The conductor takes his cracked leather seat and fits a steel lever with a wooden knob over a square peg on the control board. He pushes it one notch ahead and the outside world jerks backwards.

"Next stop, ladies and gentlemen, Hosan-ji! Hosan-ji, ladies and gentlemen. Hosan-ji if you please...."

And if *you* please, do not think me gullible to have believed her. To say that I was incredulous, sitting there while that crotchety conveyance rattled its way up the mountain, would be gross understatement. Still, it was the right button, and how can I regret now that I allowed it to be pushed?

From the hollow station, loud with rain, I passed through the turnstiles onto the sidewalk. Curtains of water fell from the eaves. The passengers from the train spread their umbrellas and ventured into the lane that glowed by the red and green light of the drink machines which lined the way to Hosan-ji temple, a popular destination when the sun was shining. Across the lane, a small red Subaru was parked next to the cutaway hillside. She had insisted she would wait for me in the car. I ducked under the drip, raced across the pavement, and folded myself into the tiny box.

The interior was dim and cramped and smelled of her perfume. She twisted around in her seat to face me. "I'm so flattered you came," she said excitedly, her eyes flashing in the half-light. She turned back to the wheel then, pulled the lapels of her coat together across her knees, and put the car into gear. I told her then, adjusting myself into a praying mantis position, that I hoped the visit would be a fruitful one. How did she know it was a pillow book? What were the distinguishing features? Was it slender or fat? How was it bound?

She concentrated on the spectres of pedestrians and road signs in the fog ahead of us. She blushed when I asked about the particulars. And you have not seen a blush until you have seen the young Ms. Ogawa perform the manoeuvre. Oh, yes, a manoeuvre it certainly is. No mere rose petals on the cheek but a wine-red flood of colour that begins at her ears, sweeps over her face, and slides down her neck, blending back into white only in the golden inverse triangle of her pendant heart. The girl's voice becomes a whisper, and she makes exaggerated use of whatever is in front of her (in this case the steering wheel, quite alarmingly). She tries to bring the world down to the level of things.

Eventually, of course, she succeeds, so let us not give undue attention to the discretions or indiscretions of chance, especially in some clichéd dormer. Of the two kinds of archaeologist, the excavator and the conservator, the latter is by far the under-appreciated. Although the excavator may be passionately committed – trowelling across desert sands, jubilantly firing his pistol into the air – one wonders if just as many great contributions to history were made by farmers' ploughs. I am being facetious, you understand, but it falls to the conservator to see the fruits of both labour and chance into the future. It is next to impossible that the original of *The Pillow Book of Lady Kasa* could have survived to the present day through the destructive heat and humidity of a thousand Japanese summers without a little help. The manuscript is certainly very old, but is not by any means an incunabulum. This has led several of my colleagues to question how an ancient text of such considerable value as literature and historical artefact could possibly have been copied and recopied for twelve centuries without ever being discovered by society at large. It is for their benefit and peace of mind that I make an hypothesis: monks.

It has often been the case in the past that the care of valuable texts was left to the church. It is more than likely, considering Nara's pre-eminence as a religious centre, that *The Pillow Book of Lady Kasa* fell into the hands (the aged, suede-soft hands) of monks at one of Nara's great temples. Impressed by the document's historic value, these scholarly monks included it in their collection of Indian and Chinese sutras, recopying it when it began to deteriorate, each new painstakingly copied text condemning the previous, a cycle of deterioration and renewal which the present conservator, suitably removed to a very amenable Skellig of the southern seas, has accepted and humbly perpetuated.

As is the case with much ancient literature, one learns little of the life of the plebeian from *The Pillow Book of Lady Kasa*. The setting is the Court, the characters are the aristocratic elite, and the concerns of the narrator are profoundly different from those of the common man. The Imperial Court was the focus of Naran society and the utmost ambition of ladies and gentlemen of some birth was to be introduced there. Kasa became one of the ladies-in-waiting to Princess Takano sometime in 745 and kept her position there until spring of 747. Her pillow book covers the last eight months of her stay at Court and includes descriptions of several well-known festivals and personages, as well as sundry, informative snippets about features of daily life. (Those familiar with the hypotheses made in my essays and articles will notice several uncanny correlations.)

A large number of Kasa's *pensées* concern her relationship with the illustrious statesman and poet, Otomo Yakamochi. He is one of the great figures of the Nara Period, having occupied several important positions at Court and contributed five hundred of his own poems (and many others which he collected from various lovers over the years) to the *Collection of 10,000 Leaves*. Unfortunately for Kasa, in September of the year 746, Yakamochi left Nara to become governor of Etchu province. Their correspondence during this time was completely one-sided: Kasa sent Yakamochi at least 29 *tanka* (now preserved in the *Collection of 10,000 Leaves*) but neither that collection nor *The Pillow Book of Lady Kasa* itself contains even one letter addressed the other way. Understandably, this left Kasa with feelings of deep despair that course beneath the surface of even her most matter-of-fact observations and give the pillow book its particular sad tinge. Having once said good-bye, Kasa and Yakamochi never met again. For reasons uncertain, she left the Court of Nara sometime in early 747, several months before Yakamochi's return, and made no more contribution to recorded history.

The arrangement of *The Pillow Book of Lady Kasa*, much like that of *The Pillow Book of Sei Shonagon*, is desultory and confusing: episodes and anecdotes follow each other with little attempt at logical or chronological sequence, there is no real sense of plot movement, and there is little attempt at conclusion or denouement. Still, it is surely the unconcerned con-catenation of event and image which is one of the book's more charming aspects. Gone is the guiding — at times dictatorial — hand of the authorial mastermind. Gone is the task of learning obscure rules to involuted literary games. Never are we left to trudge behind when the driver loads up with cargo. Nothing could be so plain and engaging and free of guile as Lady Kasa's bedtime *pensées*, light reading for those with an interest in entertainment, vital historical document for the scholar.

In *The Pillow Book of Sei Shonagon*, Mr. Ivan Morris states that "there can be no literature in the world less suited to translation than that of the classic Japanese."[7] On this point I certainly could not agree more. Working with a language which allows little or no distinction between the mutu-ally-exclusive categories we take for granted in European languages — past and present, question and affirmation, singular and plural, male and female, doubt and certainty, and, in some cases, positive and negative — the translator takes a great deal of the responsibility for the creation of meaning upon himself. The less said of this cunei-thorny issue, then, the better. On a purely grammatical level, however, there are several points about the translation that I should like to make clear. First of all, most Japanese names, except those appearing in direct quotations, appear in western order, i.e. family name second. Second, most Japanese suffixes — such as *-jo* for 'castle', *-ji* for 'temple', and *-kawa* (*-gawa*) for 'river' — have been retained, and are followed by the English equivalent in lower case; e.g. 'Hosanji temple', 'Sahogawa river' or 'Osaka-jo castle'. This practice should prove helpful to those who would follow up their reading with a visit to Japan

---

7 Morris, p. xvii

(recommended to scholars and casual readers alike), or conversation with a Japanese person, who would certainly recognise 'Todai-ji temple' but might balk at 'the Temple Todai'. Last of all, as a rule, all dates appear according to the Naran calendar, generally a month or two in advance of the Gregorian.

No further explanation of my methodologies or theories of translation will be offered here.

Any book from a civilisation as remote as eighth-century Nara would normally require a far more extensive introduction than is provided here. Had I the patience, I would certainly fill the lacunae. In lieu, I beg the reader to consider that, though he may not recognise how valuable *The Pillow Book of Lady Kasa* is to the world of historians, he may at least appreciate on an artistic level the small world it creates.

All that remains to do is to give my sincere thanks to all those who have assisted me in my travail. My gratitude goes out to innumerable friends and colleagues in Nara, Tokyo, Paris, Oxford, and Cambridge. Specifically, I owe a great deal to Mr. Philip Junta of Marcos Press, Manila, for his forbearance in editorial input, to Ms. Roxy Mandalon of Iloilo Secretarial College for typing the manuscript and this introduction, and to Professor Edwin Rommel, for the many forthcoming observations and opinions contained in his review article on *The Pillow Book of Lady Kasa,* to be published by the Luzon Journal of Asiatic Studies, vol. xxxvi, 2001.

Finally, above all, my gratitude, my thoughts, and my love go out to Marilyn Walker.

The Pillow Book of Lady Kasa

How truly now I understand
the impermanence of this world,
seeing Nara, the Imperial City,
lie thus in ruins.

On a moonlit night in the seventh month we heard the voice of a woman singing in the garden.

"Whoever could it be?" wondered the Princess, for it was late and during a period of abstinence. "Go and see who it is."

When I walked on to the veranda I saw a woman in white beside the pond. I called out to her and she came up the path through the plume grass. It was a woman in a flimsy robe, but with the moon behind her I could make out few of her features save for the sheen of moonlight on her shoulders and parted hair. She came to within several yards of me and stopped.

I asked her what she was doing outdoors at such an hour. The reply could not have been stranger:

"Snow will fall tonight," she said in a small, silvery voice. "Would you like to come outside?"

It was one of the few times that I have been truly at a loss for words. My first thought was that this was someone playing a trick, yet I would most certainly have recognised the voice had it been anyone from the palace. Standing there alone on the edge of the veranda, dressed only in my white under-robes, I felt unsteady between the ground and the wide, night sky. I took a step back.

"Would you like to come out and see the snow?" asked the woman.

All I could manage for a reply was to move my hand vaguely at my side. No, I breathed. I... am busy.

The woman turned away. Her over-robe billowed around her legs in a gust of wind and behind her the heads of plume grass shivered. I could not make up my mind what to do, and so I only watched her go as she walked back down the path towards the water. When she was gone, I went back to

Princess Takano with her strange words.

"Snow?" the Princess exclaimed in bewilderment, for it was, as I said, late in the seventh month, before the chance of snow. "Could she have been referring to falling leaves?"

I replied that there were many things which "snow" could stand for but rarely falling leaves.

"Snow in the seventh month...," she repeated absently. "Are you sure you're not just dreaming, Kasa?"

After some discussion with the other ladies we decided that the episode was beyond our comprehension. The Princess would give it no more attention and consigned it in her mind as a mere prank, the gist of which would come to light the following day.

Still, I noticed that the Princess did not sleep calmly that night. The fact of which means, of course, that neither did I.

To Otomo Yakamochi

The Kofuku-ji bell is tolling, bidding all to rest.
But you, being forever on my mind,
I cannot sleep.

How I detest

How I detest false exoticism. As if chrysanthemums or red columns were enough to imbue the most mundane scene with special significance. Rain is rain and a shadow a shadow no matter where it falls. As bad as this sentimentalism is in Chinese poetry, it is abominable in our own. In a country with few native works of literature, it is all the more obvious and distasteful.

It is the day of the Chrysanthemum Festival. On the terrace before the red columns of the Great Supreme Hall, Emperor Shomu, after tasting the saké steeped with yellow chrysanthemum petals, was presented with the ceremonial small white trouts. At that moment, just as Chamberlain Fujiwara and the Ministers of Right and Left, splendidly dressed in many-layered silks, were crossing the terrace, with the fish lined up and held aloft on Chinese mirrors, and everyone silenced by the most profound admiration, I felt a childish humour well up within me, and it was all I could do to suppress a burst of laughter.

Needless to say, I found such a reaction alarming. Later on, in her apartments, I asked Princess Takano about it. Was I sane that something so serious should cause me to laugh? To my great relief, Takano replied that this was not so strange at all. She too, she told me, putting her comb back into its drawer, had felt the same emotion several times before. Once, at the Kamo Festival of all times and places, she and the Vestal Virgin, standing side by side in front of the great shrine, surrounded with garlands of hollyhocks and all the monks hushed in prayer, had begun to giggle. It was extremely embarrassing and Chamberlain Fujiwara, among others, had grown quite red with indignation. But there was nothing either of them could do to stop giggling. Everything that seemed most serious only caused them further mirth. "Sitting in the audience at the Chrysanthemum is one thing, Kasa, but just try peeing yourself in front of everyone at Kamo!" she laughed.

The Princess is so kind. Hearing her story put me quite at ease. I took up a little knife and ventured to peel a pear.

Takano wondered if I knew the origin of the ceremony.

"Was there something we were celebrating, or lamenting, or trying to ward off?" she asked.

"Kamo or Chrysanthemum?" I asked.

"Either one, I suppose."

I had to admit that I did not know.

"I wonder if it's all just for our amusement," she said.

Such an opinion is the privilege of a princess. I myself believe there must be a worthy intent for every ceremony — practical or magical — without which there would only be spectacle. "Do you know how many ceremonies there are, Kasa?"

"There used to be one for every day," I replied, the nude, glistening white fruit now slipping about in my fingers as I tried to shear off the rest of the peel in one unbroken ribbon. "But many have disappeared, some have been amalgamated, others have sunk into routine, like raising your cup before drinking; it used to be a prayer for rain in the fifth month."

Takano found this delightful. "Really? I wonder how many ceremonies we conduct without even knowing," she whispered, as if the *kami* themselves were listening. "Careful with that pear, Kasa. It might be sacred."

Things that make a thunking sound in the night

A carriage going over the threshold at Akatainukai Gate. A clumsy visitor's wooden head-dress against the transom. The heavy bamboo water conduit in the East Precinct Garden. A stone with poem attached, landing on the floorboards of the veranda. One's pillow falling over in the midst of a vigorous dream. Quite alarming!

Princess Takano and I were sitting on the veranda sometime in the fifth month, when we saw Otomo Yakamochi walking across the yard towards the State Halls. He was elegantly dressed in green and he swung his arms at his sides as he walked, looking very pleased with himself indeed. I certainly had no intention of speaking with him, but just as he was passing by, the Princess called out to him and then scurried behind the curtain of state to leave me absolutely stuck, the only one on the veranda, and Yakamochi coming back thinking *I* had called to him. I would have followed the Princess and given her a sound scolding, but I could hardly have done it without looking like a complete fool in front of Yakamochi. He, of course, flattered to be addressed by a lady, came across the gravel into the shade of the eaves.

He was wearing a forest green head-dress — albeit one of the soft, low-crowned types — and an over-robe of a lighter fern, belted with black. His pants were a pale rose and his scabbard was of Chinese vermilion. I vividly remember the cords of his head-dress bouncing across his chest as he walked. I would simply have appreciated watching him pass by in his finery, but now I was forced to talk with the man on no pretext whatsoever.

"It's Kasa, isn't it?" he asked, peering into the veranda. "May I part the blind?"

He certainly could not. I asked him in the most derisive tone how he had possibly made such a hideous colour combination. Wasn't there some kind of standard for guards? Unaccountably, my severe demeanour seemed to put the man at ease.

"Of course there's a code," he laughed, pushing back the blind several inches so that he could take a seat on the edge of the veranda. "But my shift's over. These are my fraternising clothes." He put his hands on his knees and made no further effort to sustain a conversation.

Across the yard, the young Prince Asaka was trying to coax a white cat from underneath the veranda of the Empress Komyo's apartment. He had a ball of silk cord which he dangled in front of it, but the cat was timid. It came forward to bat at the the thing with a hesitant paw but retreated whenever Asaka tried to grab it. Yakamochi watched the young prince with amusement. At the nape of his neck, every strand of his hair was pulled up and knotted flawlessly beneath the head-dress. He was a lovely man and I found his nonchalance aggravating. "Are all the Guards' Captains as impolite as you?" I asked him finally.

At this he straightened up abruptly. "What do you mean, *all* the Guards' Captains?" he replied indignantly. "Why would there be more than one?"

"Well, who's doing your job?" I asked, and quite sensibly I felt.

"At this very moment you mean...? No one."

Until then I had never given any thought to what palace guards actually did. I had always assumed that their appearance at festivals and ceremonies was a *secondary* task. Had bandits never tried to sack the palace? or the hairy Ainu?

"Hairy Ainu!" He laughed loudly and clapped his hands with delight. "Hairy Ainu! I haven't heard that since my grandfather last waylaid me with one of his stories.... Hairy Ainu... do you want to know what I spend my time doing, Kasa? I fill out *mokkan* all day, just like any other official."

I did not appreciate Yakamochi's laughter. How should one be expected to know such things? We sat in uneasy silence. The cat fled across the yard and Asaka followed it. Yakamochi glanced back. "What were you writing?"

I folded the page that lay before me. "You *are* rude. I was helping the Princess Takano with a poem."

"A poem?" He straightened up again, this time out of curiosity. "I didn't know you were a poet."

"You still don't."

"Come now," he objected, "if you were helping Takano, you must know a little about the subject yourself."

"Who can afford not to be a poet?" I replied.

He nodded in agreement. And was silent again. If this was his 'fraternising', I wondered what he was like pensive. "Read me your poem," he said suddenly.

"I told you, silly man, that it's Takano's poem."

"If it's Takano's poem, where's Takano?"

At this point I really had had enough. I had shown adequate good manners in entertaining him and he could not expect more. "You're being a nuisance," I told him. "I never asked you to come sit on my veranda. I think you had better leave." This he did far too willingly and I was left in a mood all day.

Frustrating as the encounter was, it now seems charming to remember it.

To Otomo Yakamochi

If it were death to love,
I should die for you —
and die again,
one thousand times over.

Magnificent things

The parade of blue horses, even if they are grey. Arrows fletched with falcon. One has arrived late at a ceremony; rushing through the colonnade, one becomes aware of the unusual silence and wonders if one has been mistaken about the date. Passing through the gate, one finds a thousand people seated in the plaza, all absolutely still. A good melon. Anything from China. The Emperor's zelkova coffret. On my first day at Court I was invited to go along with Princess Takano to the Imperial Domicile to meet the Emperor. I was so nervous that I never once looked up from the floor and all I can remember is staring at that coffret, trying not to faint. The smell of cold ashes in the brazier on a rainy morning. The sun going down over Mount Ikoma. An unexpected gift. Even better, an unexpected visit.

There is the same

There is the same white cat crying in the yard. If one did not know better, one would say it was the crying of a child. I cannot see it tonight, but I have seen it on previous nights skirting the yard, ducking under the veranda when the guards pass by. I have asked Prince Asaka what name he has given to his cat, but he refuses to tell me.

To Otomo Yakamochi

Never, even in my heart,
did I imagine it:
that I would long for you like this,
although no mountains
or rivers separate us.

The statues of Kannon

The statues of Kannon, Goddess of Mercy, in the temple, resemble the people you know. Once you have recognised a face, you shall never again behold merely lifeless bronze. That cast visage, distant in its silence, even with your fingers upon it, suddenly, without warning, lives. When you return to the gallery of Kannon you are no longer a stranger, you return to it as if to your own city. All these quiet faces were crying, whispering, plotting, laughing as you approached. They only fell silent when you entered.

Rank

Four grades for Imperial Princes. Twenty-seven ranks for other mortals. After this there are only *tadabito,* commoners of no fixed existence. Rank, division, and grade are reviewed and adjusted once per year.

It has been known for someone to move up five or six ranks in his lifetime. There was one man, a carpenter of the eighteenth rank, who saved young Yuhari from a boar. Yuhari was unharmed, but the man was gored by the animal and eventually died from the wound. The Emperor, much in debt to him, appeared at his bedside and bestowed upon him the twelfth rank. At his death, this was raised to the tenth. We all agreed that it was a most remarkable career ascent.

A ruined poem

Before Princess Takano precipitated our first meeting, I had never taken any interest in Otomo Yakamochi, for all his charming looks. But from that one short introduction a curiosity grew. Nothing in his demeanour led me to believe that this interest was mutual, until he appeared one day at the East Precinct Garden.

A fabulous storm had arrived above the Land of Yamato and I was watching it from the veranda of the Small Pavilion.

There was a column of black cloud approaching from the north, and the rain was draped in violet curtains across the hillsides. I was amazed by the speed of the storm and I had the feeling that I was the only one standing before it as it rushed down the valley. So lost in thought was I, that when the rain finally did reach me, rasping across the pond and clattering against the roof tiles, I did not think to close the blinds, but only took several steps back to avoid the drops.

In the midst of the downpour the gate at the far end of the garden opened and a figure ran down the path beside the pond. When he reached the house he practically leapt onto the veranda and frightened me from my trance.

"No," he laughed, "it's not the *shikkongo shin*[1]. Just Yakamochi. The Princess told me you were here."

"So I am," I replied, trying my best to seem at ease.

"I wrote you a poem...," he continued breathlessly, "but I'm afraid the rain has ruined it."

I asked him to show it to me anyhow, but he declined. "No, it's quite ruined," he insisted. "I shall have to write another and return in more clement weather. And then you, Lady Kasa, shall have to reciprocate."

I wondered if he really had written a poem for me at all, but if not, what was he doing out in the storm? He was drenched and his robes were making a puddle where he stood. He did not stay long. Without another word, he jumped from the veranda and sprinted back down the pathway, his figure turning to grey in the steam rising from the pond.

When I returned home, Princess Takano asked me what happened. I told her that I thought Yakamochi was insane. She wanted to know if I was disappointed that there was no poem, but I could not tell. She suggested we invent the poem

---

[1] thunderbolt bearer

he might have written. At first, I was amused by her suggestion, but it turned out to be rather embarrassing in the end: I had no idea in the world what Yakamochi might have written for me.

To Otomo Yakamochi

Though we only saw each other
dimly through the morning mist,
I go on longing for you,
so much that I shall die.

One simply has to feel

One simply has to feel sorry for Lady Gorii, though she is shown exaggerated kindness by those at Court. You see, she has a growth upon her nose that reminds one, as the ancient saying goes, of 'a well-ripened fruit carried in a mountaineer's sack.'

This brush and inkstone

This brush and inkstone were a gift of Otomo Yakamochi's. The inkstone is one of the largest I have ever seen. When the princess first saw it she jumped. "Is that a tortoise you've got?" It does resemble a tortoise, I must admit, with its four clawed feet, although the back is a concave dish. It is cut from a very heavy stone, so it certainly encourages sedentary concentration. When Otomo gave it to me, long after our first meeting, I had a mind to ask why he had given me such a large one, but this would have been rude. The dark grey stone is veined with quartz that has turned indigo at the edges of the ink pool. Much as I love this stone, the brush is my favourite of Otomo's gifts. It is made of horsehair fitted to a simple length of bamboo. The joints of the bamboo fit my fingers perfectly, and if there ever comes a time when this brush must be replaced, I shall have to find one with the joints spaced just so.

Yet another hour

Yet another hour goes past without seeing you. I get up from my place overlooking the beach and begin to pace. The women here cannot stand it but I persist in spite of their complaints.

To Otomo Yakamochi

This world is thick with men's eyes,
and so I must go on longing for you,
my Lord,
though you are near to me
as the spaces in a bridge of stepping stones.

Not everyone

Not everyone has the good fortune to be beautiful, but every face has something to recommend it. Even the ugliest person, I find, has some admirable feature that one may appreciate. When I am in conversation with someone who is ugly, I do my best to concentrate upon whichever feature is not particularly offensive, and appreciating it brings me genuine joy. So I am watching Lady Gorii's dimples appear and disappear as she speaks, or the Minister of Trade's long eyelashes, or the slight, shiny, inward curve of the Rector Nishiyama's temples. Only in speaking with the Chamberlain Fujiwara is my every effort foiled and I am forced to look at his pointed silk shoes.

When the officials are getting changed into court dress and taking their breakfast at the Morning Assembly Halls, I like to pass through and watch them. Here there are many lower officials mixed with those of higher rank and it is impossible to tell which is which when they first arrive. Only when they are dressed in their robes does one learn their rank and wonder however such and such a man, who had looked so dignified before, could be a mere scribe.

Last spring, a new stone

Last spring, a new stone was placed in the East Precinct Garden. Since then, we have all become most fond of it for its pleasing shape and distinctive character. Emperor Shomu decided yesterday that the stone has healing properties and deserves court rank.[2] In a small ceremony, during which the stone was bathed and girded with a woven rope, the Emperor gave it the name 'Healer' and elevated it to the Tenth Rank. Lord Tabito suggested it be given a government post as well and Emperor Shomu replied sprightly, "Yes, yours."

We all found this very amusing. Tabito has a reputation for the most exceptional laziness.

On the fourth day of the second month

On the fourth day of the second month in the same year, we saw Lady Kannagibe Maso, the Great Vestal Virgin, pass

---

[2] It was not uncommon in the Nara Period for inanimate objects, fauna, and flora to hold court rank. Cats, bows, hats, melons, pillows, and inkstones were some of the lucky beneficiaries of Imperial promotion. Nostalgic as I was at the sight of your things, your cat was very soon the beneficiary of a Walkerian demotion out-of-doors. Don't worry, Casper did not hang on the screen for long. He and that little boy next door were getting on famously when I left.

by on her way to Kamo Shrine for the Festival of the Spring Prayer. Many Shinto officials went there with her to carry out rituals and recite prayers for a good harvest in the coming year. They were dressed in their dark black silks with mauve embroidery, and upon their heads they wore the tall cones that have to be tied tight beneath the chin when there is a wind. As they passed through the gravel yard between the Princess's and the Empress's apartments, they clapped their wooden sticks together to clear the air around the Virgin. Sitting in my room together, Princess Takano and I commented on how lovely the Virgin was in her layered silks, each of a successively deeper green, until the edge of the last robe made a bright red rim around her ankles. Such an honour to be chosen the Great Vestal! But such a pity as well; she is a lovely girl and there would be a great many men willing to court her otherwise.[3]

I first came

I first came to have a notebook when Otomo brought me one. I am always very pleased to have some new paper, especially when it is coloured paper, or decorated, or even a plain white paper if it is nice. This was the first that I had received a notebook and I was overcome with pleasure at the sight of it.

"Now you must write a diary in a careful hand," Otomo told me, "and record all of your poems in it. One day I should like to read it."

---

[3] *Lady Kannagibe Maso, to Otomo Yakamochi*

> Did you hear
> the voice of the wild goose
> as it flew above,
> crying as she sought her mate?
> Oh what a plaintive sound.

To Otomo Yakamochi

Oh how steadily I love you —
you who awe me
like the thunderous waves
that lash the sea coast of Isé!

Nara palace

We have all come to stay at the West Palace for Princess Takano's monthly defilement. None of us likes it here because the building is old and centipedes keep falling from the ceiling. When the Princess asked us to recite a poem my choice was the most fitting of anyone's. I asked the Princess if she remembered her father's folly in moving the capital to Kuni, and then I recited the poet Sakimaro's lament:

O Nara, city of my abiding trust!
Because the times are new,
all have gone — led by their sovereign —
even as the spring flowers fade,
or as the crows fly away at evening.
On its wide streets where once proudly walked,
the lords and ladies of the Great Palace,
no horses pass; nor men.
What desolation — alas!

Now that with the change of times,
Nara is become,
an Imperial City that was,
the grass grows rank in the streets.[4]

---

[4] De Bary, Ed., p. 121.

I, for one, give no city my abiding trust. I love Nara only inasmuch as it is possible to love a place, which is a shallow kind of attachment at best. One need not look far to find ten poems by the same author praising the capitals of Fujiwara, Nara, Naniwa, Shigaraki, Kuni, and Nara again, each as if it were the one and only love of his life. A person may stop and wait for you in time. No place ever stops unless it is forced, and I have more faith in myself than in carpenters.

I will now describe Nara Palace:

The entire compound of the Imperial Palace of Nara measures ten *cho* east to west and eight *cho* north to south. [1.1 km^2 with an eastern extension of 0.8 x 0.3 km that was in dispute for some time and only positively verified after excavations for a highway project revealed ancient architectural features.] There are ten gates in the great outer wall. On the southern side, from west to east, are Wakainukai Gate [also called 'Music Bureau' Gate], Scarlet Phoenix Gate at the centre, Mibu Gate, and, where East 1st Column Avenue meets 2nd Row Middle Avenue, Chiisako Gate. On the eastern wall are those closest to the Imperial Domiciles, Yamabe and Akatainukai Gates. On the northern wall there is only one gate; this is Ikai Gate, at the very centre. Facing the west, from north to south, are Ifukube, Saeki, and Tamate Gates.

[Of all these gates, Scarlet Phoenix was by far the most elaborate, an imposing two-storey structure with hip-gable roof and green ceramic tiles like those of the State Halls. Elegant red Chinese pillars stood in three rows of six each, spaced equidistantly, and separated by seventeen *shaku* — 5.5 metres. The base of the gate was three steps tall, made of packed earth fronted by slabs of granite, the origin of which, I believe, was not the quarry at Awaji but...5]

To Otomo Yakamochi

Could I ever forget you,
as long as my life be safe?
No, not even if my longing
increases day by day.

That evening there was a banquet

That evening there was a banquet held in the North Palace Garden. This is a lovely spot with a stream, built in the Chinese 'downstream' fashion, that wells out of rocks at one end and winds through the garden. It is covered in water lilies and there are banks of reeds and plume grass along the shoreline, a small sandy beach, and various large rocks to represent islands. Interspersed throughout the garden are black pine, plum, and sandalwood trees, and also an ancient damson in one corner that looks as if it is dying. All along the fences to the south and north are a great many more trees, placed there to conceal the fence and give an impression of continuing space beyond. Located at the west side of the garden is the pavilion, and along the east is a fence lined only with fringed pinks. Whenever I visit this garden, I am charmed by the way in which it seems to borrow the view of

---

5 The intricate geographical description which follows may be tedious to some readers. In the casual reader's interest, I have included instead a simple aerial map from *What is Japanese Architecture?*, a delightful book that anyone with an interest in the evolution of Japanese architecture would be well advised to read. The reader may wish to consult this map (Figure 4) from time to time for practical matters, or simply to imagine a tiny, lovelorn Lady Kasa strolling down the empty lanes, reclining beneath the cottonball trees, or kneeling down to watch microscopic goldfish from the bridge at bottom right.

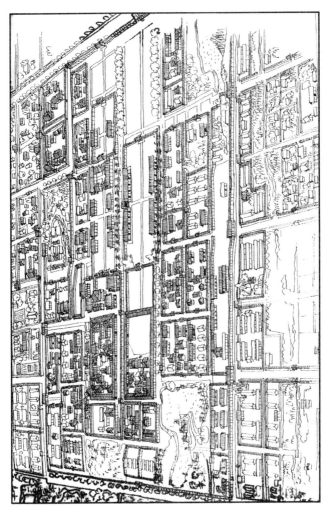

4. Nara Palace, AD 750.

the hills, as if this stream were a real river and those islands a hundred times larger than they really were. When the guests begin floating cups down the stream I can truly believe that I am standing upon a high mountain, looking down from a great perspective at the traffic upon a great river.

We arrived after dark because Princess Takano had changed her robes at the last minute and, in order to complement her, all the ladies-in-waiting were forced to do the same. I was distressed at the delay, for I was anxious to speak with Otomo about a matter that had come to my attention.

5. Reconstruction of the North Palace Garden

When we came down the path from the gate the fire huts had already been lighted and I could see several people already racing cups upon the stream. Everywhere across the lawns, people were lounging on mats surrounded with tiered lacquer dinner boxes and jugs of saké. At the south end of the pavilion, standing on the grass in front of the veranda,

Otomo was speaking with his cousin, the Lady Sakanoé's Elder Daughter.[6] I stayed in the shadows beside the gate and watched, awaiting an opportunity to approach. I heard a great oath sworn behind me then, and I turned around to find Lord Tabito laid out beneath a sandalwood tree, his feet splayed out before him. With him were the poet Sakimaro and Statesman Tachibana Moroé.

It was obvious, right away, that the three were drunk.

"Well, well, Lord Tabito," I said sternly, standing above him with my arms crossed. "You must be in a storytelling mood."

He propped himself up on his elbows and squinted at me. "Kasa? Why, Kasa. Saki! Tachi! You know Kasa, one of Takano's ladies."

Sakimaro is a narrow little man with bad vision. He has several tailors in his employ and his robes are always of the very finest quality, though he himself is a rather worn, piebald old thing. He sat cross-legged on the lawn and waved his cup at me with a silly giggle. As for Moroé, well, what does one need to say of Moroé? He was removing layers of a dinner box, looking for something to eat, just as one would have expected.

"You have good timing, Kasa," Tabito chirped happily. "Sakimaro and Tachibana and myself were just launching into a little poetry contest on the merits of saké. It's my turn, but I'll defer to you if you wish."

Graciously, I declined. "How can I describe Mount Fuji when I have never seen it?" I said, in reference to that famous poem.

---

6 *Lady Sakanoé's Elder Daughter, to Otomo Yakamochi*

> **Not a day goes by
> in which the mist does not rise
> on Mt. Kasuga.
> Likewise it is you, my love
> whom I long to see every day.**

Tabito laughed at the comparison, but Moroé, who had found a dish of beans and was now laying back on the grass, picking them out one by one with his fingers[7], snorted so loudly that I thought he had taken one of them up his nose.

"Very well, then," said Tabito. "I shall take my turn. Listen and weep, my friends. I take no responsibility for your tears." At this, he pushed himself into a half-seated position, rubbed his eyes, and holding his cup out before him told us this poem: *"Ceasing to live this wretched life of man, O that I were a saké jar! Then I should be soaked in saké! When I look upon a man,"* he continued, *"who drinks no saké, how like an ape he is! Far better, it seems, than uttering pompous words, and looking wise, to drink saké and weep drunken tears."*

Moroé snorted another bean up his nose and Sakimaro giggled into his cup. I had to admit, it was an amusing poem and Tabito all the funnier when telling it, so earnest, as if to be a clay jug were the height of anyone's ambition. "Here Kasa, sit, I'll find you a pillow."

Of course, I remained standing.

"Speaking of pillows," Moroé said, still concentrating on his dish of red beans. "Who's resting his head on yours these days, Kasa? Tabito's boy perhaps?"

Sakimaro burst into giggles again.

"How forward you are, Tachibana," I replied. "I hope the Ainu teach you some manners down in Kyushu."

Moroé slurped the juice from the bottom of the dish, now emptied of beans. When it was gone, he went back and rummaged through the lunch box. He found several oranges and tossed one to Tabito. "Here, tell Kasa to peel that for me in one go. It's a little test."

Tabito disregarded it. "Who's that woman with my son,

---

[7] Chopsticks had only recently appeared in Japan and were not widely used.

Kasa?" he asked, pointing across the garden. I turned around to find that Sakanoé's Elder Daughter had gone and Otomo's aunt, the Lady Sakanoé[8] herself, was now speaking with him. They were leaning against the veranda drinking saké from large cups. It seemed that Lady Sakanoé was chastising him. I will not hesitate to write that I quite detest Lady Sakanoé. Whenever she speaks, she does so as if imparting the most important secrets in the world, when really she is only telling you of some trifle.

"It's your own sister, Tabito," Moroé grunted. "What a parade of women to see Yakamochi, hey Kasa?"

While it appeared that Lady Sakanoé was greatly flustered, Otomo watched her gesticulate with the most placid half-smile, as if he were listening to a child. Finally he came to life to placate her and she left him for a group of women standing nearby. Seeing him alone, I took a sliver of dried shark from the tray and walked across the lawn. Just as I was approaching, though, Prince Yuhara kneeled down at the corner of the veranda and called to him. I would have turned around and left, but Otomo had already seen me coming.

"Well, Yakamochi," Prince Yuhara asked, "have you thought of a title for this little poetry collection of yours?"

"Little?" Otomo exclaimed, setting his cup down on the veranda's edge. "You have no clue, Yuhara. I'll have ten thousand pages before I'm through. Some of them will come from Kasa here, if she'll deign to be included."

"My poetry is very poor," I replied.

"Not true, not true. I know you have talents."

---

[8] *Lady Sakanoé, to Otomo Yakamochi*

This is a land of fearful gossip
so do not show your emotion.
Do not let blushing betray our love
Even if the longing kills you.

Prince Yuhara raised his eyebrows. "Talents? I can surmise." Thankfully, he did not.

When he had gone, Otomo and I stood in silence. At the south end of the garden, the light of one of the fire boxes played upon the undersides of the paulownia leaves. I watched them glitter. "Well, I've finally found a spot in the parade.... I heard something recently, Otomo. They say you are to be considered for governor of somewhere or other. And you might actually be interested."

"Kasa," he replied, "let me tell you a story."

I sighed. "I'd rather you didn't try to mitigate the truth, Otomo."

"Just listen, Kasa."

"Tell me the truth," I insisted.

"Do you know the story of the two brothers and the Chinese frieze?"

"No. And I don't want to."

"In Chang'an, not so very long ago, lived two brothers who were master stonemasons. By their twenty-first year they should have found brides and started families, but their particular devotion to their calling preceded all else and the boys remained without wives. When construction of the temple at the palace was started, a master stonemason was needed to lay the frieze under the eaves of the dome. One of the brothers was called upon by the master architect to take the job, but the young man refused to do it unless his brother too was included in the contract. The request was granted and the two young men set out for the palace. And when they came there, they were amazed.

"Now, in dividing the work, the two brothers decided to start at the same point and continue in opposite directions, laying stones until they should meet up again at the other side. They measured the circumference of the dome, agreed upon a fitting pattern, and set about their task, breaking large chunks of marble and jade with mallets, chipping away with finer, tapered hammers until the stones were perfectly round, the size of a fingernail, ready to be inserted into the design. Verily, the two brothers were so dedicated to their work that once they had begun they never left the scaffolding of the temple. They took their meals on high, and looked down upon the dusty city. They slept in hammocks strung from beams in the eaves. So grand was the great hall of Chang'an and so intricate the work the two brothers did — friezes within friezes and decorated with all manner of stylised creatures — it kept them busy for ten straight years.

"After the first five years, however, the Emperor grew impatient. The two stonemasons were the only ones not to have finished. So it was that the opening ceremonies took place while the brothers were still at work on the frieze. They looked down upon the straight squadrons of soldiers and the crowds pouring around them, and watched the fireworks exploding in the air before the dome, and wondered what the occasion could be. Likewise there were those among the crowds who gazed up at the temple and noticed the fine fili-gree of a scaffold beneath the eaves, and a spider clinging there, and wondered what it could be."

A voice spoke up: "What's this about a frieze?" I turned around to find Lord Tabito standing above us. He put his cup down on the veranda and looked curiously at his son. "What's this about a Chinese frieze?"

"Nothing," answered Otomo curtly.

"I was just curious," said Tabito. "Sounds familiar."

Otomo was stern. "Not now Father, you're drunk." I felt sorry for this man, who had probably never been as severe with his sons as they now were with him. He raised his hands in apology and turned around to leave.

"Your cup, Lord Tabito," I reminded him.

"So," Otomo continued brusquely, "there were all manner of stylised flowers and animals in the frieze, but these had all been foreseen in the plan, and though the two brothers were a hundred yards, and years apart, one working in the sunshine, the other in the shade, yet their friezes, which were actually one and the same frieze, were identical. They could not see each other, nor speak with each other, yet they were bound by the chain that stretched between them, and only by entertaining doubt could the chain be broken. If the pattern of the frieze were to alter in the slightest, it would not match up when they reached the other side and all their devotions would go to waste...."

Of course I saw the meaning of the story; I had seen it when it begun. But all I could think of was, "Ten years?"

"Oh goodness sakes, no," Otomo reacted. "I'm not spending ten years in the provinces. Perhaps one. It will be good for me. I might even find some idylls written by country-folk."

"Then the rumour was true."

Another man would have looked at his feet or toyed with his cup. Otomo looked me straight in the eyes and shrugged. "Can I come see you tonight?"

"You're unconscionable."

"Yes, I am. But can I still come see you?"

I know very well what answer I should have given him, to save myself the suffering.

To Otomo Yakamochi

Look on my tokens
and remember me.
I too shall think of you
as the years trail away
like a strand of rough gems.

A new lady-in-waiting

Lady Nakatomi's sudden decision to marry the Rector Nishiyama has stunned us all. Nishiyama is rather old and stooped; some say his brothers used to force him to pick rice with the commoners. I, for one, never thought Nakatomi would marry him. But there has been rumour that a short-term affair with one man or another has ended with a foreseeable consequence, and she is now in a great hurry to be married. Of course, old Nishiyama will be delighted. He will strut about for a time, and take up hunting again, boasting that his arrows are still sharp, until he learns the truth and drops dead at his own feet.[9] All very convenient for Lady Nakatomi, but inconvenient for the rest of us. Her departure leaves only four ladies in attendance to Princess Takano: Ki, Heguri, Gorii, and I. For the daughter of the Emperor it is not proper that she have an even number in her retinue, so a new lady-in-waiting will arrive in one month to replace her.

The new lady-in-waiting

The new lady-in-waiting has finally come. Her name is Koto. She is young and very pretty and we all hope that she will get along well. So often it is difficult for a young girl to

---

[9] Women of the Nara Period were ever ready to carry on sentimental adventures whenever they found opportunities, and the gentlemen of the time were not disposed to discourage them altogether. Perhaps, in this respect, not much has changed in 1200 years. The truth was, of course, that another man was the father of Lady Nakatomi's child namely:

Lady Nakatomi to Otomo Yakamochi

Should you refuse me,
do you think I would force you?
No, I would remain
confused in love as the roots of rush
and still keep longing for you.

adjust to court life. I, myself, had so many strange, romantic ideas about court life. Even after a month with Princess Takano, I was still blushing when the guards walked past in the night, pulling their bow strings to ward off spirits. The first time I saw a guard, I thought he was a courtier playing an instrument and had come to serenade me. Such ideas!

The Big Buddha.[10]

Construction of the *Daibutsu* continues and everyone includes it in their prayers. I heard Emperor Shomu say that when it is completed it will be of such grand scale that a man may climb through the nostril. Today I took Koto up the hill to see the progress.

Much has changed since I was in these hills last. On a flat, cleared expanse where there had only been forest before there are many, many men at work on the construction of the Todai-ji temple. There is a complex of workshops and shacks as big as a village, surrounded by a constant stream of labourers and cart traffic. The noise is thunderous. Only the foundation of the temple has been laid, but one can see that it will be immense. Beyond the workshops and piles of stone and logs and sawyer's rigs, we could see a scaffold rising above the trees with a roof of thatch on top of it. We ordered the carriage to go over there, and when we came near we were greeted with the oddest, most impressive sight of all. Resting on great wooden blocks, surrounded by a scaffold of bamboo, were the monstrous bronze haunches and belly of the Buddha. We could see many squared lines upon his 'skin' where the panels of cast bronze had been fitted

[10] The *Daibutsu* ['Big Buddha'] is the largest gilt bronze Buddha in the world and the temple which houses it, the Todai-ji, the world's largest wooden building. A model of permanence, it still stands (if you were wondering) just to the west of our old house.

together. Many men were at work here, clambering over the massive legs with brushes, hammers and other tools. The master architect, Kuninaka no Muraji Kimimaro, in his tall black head-dress, stood on one of the knees with his long-stick in his hand, calmly watching the progress. Above him, where the chest and shoulders of the Buddha should have been, was a mere framework of wood and wax, unclothed as yet by the shining cast panels.

Before this strange sight were many more sawyer's rigs, piles of material, balks of building timber being pulled toward the site, and smoking cauldrons. Koto and I stayed in our carriage watching for a long time. The cauldron fires had begun to glow in the falling light before we realised it was time to go home. The carpenters passing by made dark silhouettes against the sparks. The yelling subsided and we heard laughter instead. In the west, Mount Ikoma was outlined against the sky, growing larger and darker until it seemed as if the sun had crept up right behind it and was

6. Todai-ji temple

casting its crimson light straight up to the clouds. O wondrous and comforting is Mount Ikoma, Protector of the Land of Yamato and the glorious City of Nara!

Koto and I agreed to write poems for Mount Ikoma when we returned and present them to the Princess to tell her of the beautiful view. When we wanted to return, I had to reach through the shutter and pinch the driver who was asleep.

As we started down the hill we could see to the south where the dull orange trails of the Horokawa rivers drifted across the rice land and disappeared into the shadows of the mountains of Kai. The view was perfected when Koto pointed out the twin five-storied pagodas of Yakushi-ji, still visible below us in the middle distance. Unaccountably, this view gave me a melancholy feeling, and when we got back I refused to write my poem after all. Koto was upset. Poor girl. She is young and so easily disappointed. She has no idea at all what the night can be like.

To Otomo Yakamochi

More sad thoughts crowd into my mind
when evening comes; for then appears your phantom shape —
speaking as I have known you speak.

A great box of crabs

A great box of crabs arrived from the port at Naniwa today. We went to see them at the Inner Catering Office and the top layer was still alive. It gave me an uneasy feeling. We decided to set one free in the western pond to see if it would survive. Nonchalantly, as if she did it every day, Lady Koto carried it trapped between two slats of wood that she held before her like an offering. We must have looked a strange procession walking past the west palace, four skittish ladies following young Koto and a quivering blue crab.

The cooks had said it would die in fresh water, but we wanted to see for ourselves. Koto dropped it into the shallow water by Pebble Beach. I thought it would die immediately, but it only sank to the bottom and rested calmly on the pebbles, occasionally lifting a claw, moving to the left or the right, but never going anywhere. We soon got tired of it and decided to leave. We would come back tomorrow and if it were still alive we would tell everyone that the pond had a resident crab. We would call it Kaniko.

Lady Heguri, who had been the most frightened of it, felt compelled to ask how long a crab lived.

None of us could honestly say. How long does a crab live? Then Koto called out to us.

We all turned and stared at the crab. It had begun to panic. It tried to climb an invisible wall towards the surface but once it got there it only struggled frantically — "Kaniko the dancing crab!" Koto cried out, which I thought was heartless, for the creature was obviously dying.

The crab's panic was soon over. Its movement lapsed. It sank back under the water and came to rest upside down on the stones, its wrinkled white bottom staring up to the surface like a face.

To Otomo Yakamochi

Like the crane that cries
merely to be heard from afar
in the dark of night,
must I only hear from you?
Will we never again get to meet?

Sometimes I find

Sometimes I find life in the palace to be so cloistered! It is like living in a country of foreigners. And, though I understand the words these people say, I do not understand their problems. Nor can they understand mine. To be a frustrated lover is to be a fugitive.

An overheard conversation

An overheard conversation is a wonderful bit of luck. Going out of one's way to eavesdrop is, of course, quite reprehensible, but if people are careless enough to speak of private matters in another's presence it is certainly no fault of the listener. On the third day of the third month Empress Komyo threw a private 'Banquet of the Stream'.[11] It was held in honour of Statesman Tachibana Moroé, whom I had already had the pleasure of meeting at a similar party only shortly before. He had just been appointed the newest Governor General of the Dazaifu down in Kyushu, and everyone from the palace was invited to take part in the festivities. For many of the statesmen these banquets are especially happy times, for they know that they themselves are safe from the Dazaifu appointment for another year. For my own part, I was certainly glad to know that Moroé was leaving, but I happened to be suffering from an infection then and I was

---

[11] A quasi-ritual social occasion imported from China. People would gather to improvise poems and to float cups of wine on a flowing stream. A good idea of the fun involved can be had by visiting Arugo restaurant in Shinsaibashi, Osaka [See Figure 7]. The bar faces a kind of trough and delicacies of all kinds come floating past on sturdy little wooden boats. I remember watching you have no end of fun writing ridiculous notes for downstream diners. You may not have known it at the time, but this was not so different from the old custom of setting poetry afloat. The idea was to follow one's lover's cup amidst the throng of them and then retrieve it downstream.

hardly in the mood to walk about, much less make useless conversation with the drunken revelers sure to be splayed across the lawns.

When the other ladies went into the banquet, I stayed behind in my palm-leaf carriage and watched the festivities from just beyond the gate.

At sunset, as the sky above Mount Ikoma was turning a brilliant shade of orange, I saw two figures approaching the gate. Presuming there was no one left sitting in the rows of carriages pulled up in the gravel lot just outside, Princess Takano and Otomo's cousin, Lady Sakanoé's Elder Daughter,[12] came out to the gate to speak in private. Princess Takano seemed concerned.

"Whatever for?" I heard her ask.

"You can't guess?" Sakanoé's Elder Daughter replied incredulously. "Really, I don't know how you can be so naive, Princess. We've sent dozens of letters in only four weeks...."

Takano still looked confused. My curiosity too was piqued.

"Well, marriage!" the girl cried out happily. "He's asked me to marry him."

It was obvious that Princess Takano was stunned. She put her hand to her forehead and leaned back against the open door of the gate. The girl continued: "I know he has a reputation, but he's changed now. I can hear it in his poems." The Princess was silent. Sakanoé's Elder Daughter reacted with alarm. "Do you not advise it?" she asked quickly. "Am I making the wrong decision?"

---

[12] *Lady Sakanoé's Elder Daughter, to Otomo Yakamochi*

> Brave man, I realize
> you have yearned for me,
> but could your longing compare
> to that in the heart
> of a frail-limbed woman?

7. Arugo Restaurant

At this, Princess Takano awakened from her surprise. She came forward from her stance against the gate and put her arms out to the other lady. "Of course not, dear," she managed. "He's a fabulous character, absolutely illustrious...."

Just then a great cheer went up in the garden. The fire boxes were being lighted and sparks swarmed into the evening sky. My entertainment came to a sudden end. Princess Takano and Lady Sakanoé's Elder Daughter walked back down the gravel path to the stream where everyone was gathering. It was the last I heard of their conversation.

I always enjoy the chance to inform Otomo of events at court. That very night, I wrote a letter informing him of Sakanoé's Elder Daughter's impending marriage and the manner by which I had overheard it.[13]

---

[13] Kasa's naivete seems incredible to us, but I, for one, can sympathize.

To Otomo Yakamochi

Are my thoughts
revealed to others?
I dreamed my jewelled comb box
was opened to the light.

Double-edged things

An invitation to State Halls. Lady Sakanoé's brush. A fine morning on a day of confinement. Just about anything Lady Koto says. Her naivete is charming, but at the same time too objective. She asked me just now why I write "such feeble poems to Yakamochi all the time."

"Feeble?" I repeated, exercising great restraint.

"It seems to me that you could take just about anything and make it an image of your love," she said. "This bowl of beans, for instance. Or that ox... 'Like the ox, I labour at this —'"

"Koto!"

"Like the sweaty ox, I moan for —"

"Koto!" I reached across the brazier and slapped her arm. "You should not make fun of what you do not understand. This is what you do when you're in love."

"That's 'what you do?'" she repeated. "As if it were some sort of obligation?"

"It *is* an obligation."

"Then you don't mean what you write."

"Of course I do. Maybe if it weren't a social obligation, as you put it, I would never realize what I truly feel." A snowfall when one is out of doors. A great deal of leisure. A tropical paradise.

The Princess's domicile

The house in which we live is three bays wide by five bays

long. It is surrounded by covered verandas. The western veranda faces the yard and is generally much busier than the eastern veranda, with attendants, ministers, and ladies-in-waiting passing along the stone walkways, to and from the Emperor's domicile, the Empress's domicile, and the Catering offices.

Our house is composed of one large room partitioned by bamboo and lacquer screens, and curtains hung from movable wooden frames. These are staggered throughout the room to create chambers and corridors; above them, one can see the rafters of the roof from one end of the house to the other. Whenever there are gentlemen visitors who wish to remain unknown, they remove their head-dresses before entering, so as not to be seen by anyone peering overtop.

I remember once when Otomo's father, Lord Tabito, came to talk with me, he could not find the proper path through all the partitions and yelled out that he was lost. I stood up from where I was sitting and I could see his tall head-dress moving around above the curtain frames.

"What a maze you women live in!" he cried when he finally reached me, and then whispered: "I was afraid I was going to stumble across Lady Gorii somewhere back there."

Lady Ki occupies the northern end of the room. Ladies Heguri and Gorii, the central portion, and Koto and I the south. Lady Ki has the prettiest screens of any of us, all of them gifts from the numerous gentlemen she has known in her long period of service.[14]

---

14 *Lady Ki, to Otomo Yakamochi*

I have entwined the threads of my life
into a true lovers' knot,
so another time, I'm sure,
I shall see you once again.

8. The Princess's Domicile

In the summertime the domiciles are much more pleasant than any of the official buildings roofed with tiles in the Chinese style. Of course, the tiles' green tinge is far more attractive to look at than thatch, especially from a distance, from Kasuga Field for instance, when the roofs of the palace seem to shimmer like water. But they collect so much heat during the day that it makes these buildings all but unbearable. Were you to go into the State Halls or the Great Supreme Hall of a summer afternoon you would find it entirely deserted. Homes should be built for the summer. In the winter one can live anywhere, but dwellings unsuited to the hot months are unendurable.

To Otomo Yakamochi

As long as you are near
I can live without seeing you,
but if you go farther away,
I fear I cannot bear it.

Soon after Otomo's departure Tabito went down to pay a visit to Yoshino. When he returned he came to visit. We sat next to the brazier and he told me the strangest of stories. While he was there, drinking saké in the pleasant rooms of the upper palace and composing poems to celebrate the fall colours, there came into the house a bearded man dressed in such finery that the other men marveled at his appearance.

"On top of flowered orange trousers he wore three under-robes of unlined silk and a doubled black and red over-robe with a pattern of hollyhocks bordered by a golden Chinese frieze. He wore a tall court head-dress and a magnificent scabbard of worked silver that shone in the light of the candles.

"He entered the room without introducing himself and knelt down on the mat to pick up a bowl. He poured this bowl full from a nearby jug and, holding it high for all to see, swiftly inverted it. The lady of the house gasped. But, much to everyone's amazement, nothing fell. The bowl was empty.

"Well, you can imagine. All the men in the house burst out into cheers and laughter, assuming that it was some form of entertainment that had been arranged for them.

"So, to emphasize his feat, the man filled the bowl again and as he had done the first time turned it upside-down above the floor. And again the bowl was empty. He repeated

---

[15] This entry is suspect. Tabito led a brilliant military career and was much renowned as a poet. More importantly here, he was the father of Otomo Yakamochi, Lady Kasa's lover. Unfortunately, Tabito died in the year 731, 16 years before Lady Kasa's pillow book was even written. This entry, and others mentioning Tabito, have not been extracted from the present edition because, first of all, Tabito is rather charming, Khayyam-esque, rotund as his name; and, secondly, because his presence demonstrates the cumulative, malleable nature of history. The past, the archaeologist soon learns, is rarely as safe as when it is beneath the soil. When it passes through men's hands it is likely to be smudged. And this is Tabito, a smudge, delightful as he may be. To remove him and every other suspect entry in the pillow book might very well leave us with nothing.

the trick several times, always refilling his bowl from the same jug. Then, when the jug was finally empty, the bearded man put down the bowl and lifted the jug on high instead. This provoked sudden mirth, for we all expected that he would invert the empty jug as he had done the cups and that this time, conversely, it would be full."

Here, Tabito paused to take a drink from his own cup and filled it twice over, as if storytelling made him thirsty. "Now where was I? The bearded man... was he bearded?"

"Yes."

"Yes, of course. The bearded man in his fabulous trousers and splendid over-robe is kneeling before his audience with the jug held high above his head. All are waiting in silence, overcome by the tension he has created by his silent show. At this moment a smile comes over his face, for the audience is his alone. But his eyes do not smile. He watches sternly the men seated around him, holding them powerless. He reaches up with his free hand and perches the base of the jug precariously upon his fingertips. The vessel, which everyone assumes to be full, though they have seen with their own eyes that it is empty, is wavering in the air. Upon the flared mouth, glistening in the light of the tapers burning in the room, a drop of steely liquid trembles."

And then Tabito groaned. He lifted his weight from the floor. "I'm afraid I have to be going now, Kasa," he said.

"What?!" I cried.

"Yes, I am sorry but I do have to return home for dinner. The women will be upset if I'm late."

"But the jug!" I protested. "What about the strange man and the jug?"

Tabito shuffled towards the door, wedging his ivory *mokkan* down into his sash. "Oh that," he said nonchalantly. "My son and I are good storytellers, aren't we? You should learn not to be taken in by such fancy tales." And with that he left the room. He groaned again as he stepped down from the veranda. I listened incredulously to his footsteps across the gravel and, several minutes later, the greeting call of the guards at the eastern middle gate.

Mumyo

The young Prince Asaka adores the cats in the palace and became worried when he noticed Mumyo fattening. He wondered if the Inner Catering Bureau were feeding her too much. It was charming to listen in as Princess Takano explained to him that she was pregnant.

Koto has decided that she will only

Koto has decided that she will only play a *koto* made of paulownia wood. She saw Emperor Shomu playing one which he had received from China and she decided that she no longer cared for the one she had. Of course, her instructor from the Music Bureau was furious.

"How can she make such demands?" he cried at me, standing on my veranda with the rejected *koto* in his hand. Of course, I had already heard from Koto everything that had gone on between them and decided not to get involved. I hardly care for the fact that every time Koto does something to infuriate, discomfort, or insult someone, they come to me for an explanation. I am her housemate, after all, not her mother. And Fujiwara is the worst. He comes to me repeatedly, complaining that Koto is too ornery or cold — "always blowing east one day and west the next" — and that it is *my* duty to see that she behaves.

I told the music instructor to let her play a paulownia *koto* if that was what she wanted.

The music instructor sprayed saliva across my robes. "Why doesn't she just play a golden one!" he cried. "Do you think I can just go down to the East Market and pick one up for a couple of coins? She says if she can't play a paulownia harp, then she will only play *sho*."

"Then let her play *sho*," I replied.

"She *can't* play *sho*! *Sho* is only for men to play. It's not a woman's instrument. It's not proper."

Really, it was all I could do to get the exasperated man off my veranda. I have an idea that Koto finally got her way, though. I heard someone playing *sho* very badly on the west veranda several evenings ago.

The Festival of the Young Herbs

When you arrive at the Festival of the Young Herbs, you may not notice that there is a festival going on at all. All that will be seen are women and men in everyday dress picking herbs from the meadows on Nara Hill. Here and there are officials from the Imperial Storehouse, collecting what is found. They go about their work quietly and seriously, searching through the grasses for the seven lucky herbs. By morning's end there are several baskets full. These are taken to the Inner Catering Office, where they are stewed with rice to make gruel, a bowl of which is offered to the Emperor.

In the early morning

In the early morning I open the door several inches to get the air. It is still dark under the eaves of the houses but the sky is beautifully illuminated. The edge of the veranda is wet with dew and so are the stone walks. Above the water the hills

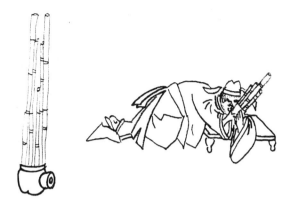

9. *sho* (thirteen-pipe flute)

of Panay look like sleeping animals with their heads tucked under. A file of fruit bats beats home from the mainland, where they have been feeding in the mango plantations by night. I could not stand to live up in the village, with such commotion every morning. Here on the beach, the morning creeps in like a favourite tawny cat. It nuzzles and rubs against you with its soft fur, and for a few dreamy minutes you look admiringly upon it before going back to sleep.

The Great Purification

Few ceremonies are as demanding as the Great Purification. "An assembly of Imperial Princes and officials, who have attained ritual purity by fasting and continence, gather by the main gate of the Imperial Palace and perform a Shinto service to purge all His Majesty's subjects of their impurity and sin.... In addition, a life-sized figure of the Emperor is washed in a river, so that all Imperial impurities may be removed."[16]

---

[16] Morris, p. 162.

Emperor Shomu has many, many scrolls. If all the scrolls in his collection were put on display there would not be a bare wall in the entire palace. The Emperor likes very much to look through these things when he is not studying scripture. He admires the *imamekashi* ['in vogue'] Chinese craftsmanship and occasionally sets out a piece in the State Halls for everyone to admire. To come to my point — which is the foolishness of Chamberlain Fujiwara — the Emperor decided to display a scroll in the East Precinct Garden for a recent banquet. This particular scroll was received from a Chinese ambassador. It depicts an amorous scene from a text called the *Yü Fang Pi Chüeh* ['Secret Prescriptions of the Bedchamber'] and because of its subject matter was hung in the Small Pavilion across the pond from the Main Pavilion.

When we arrived and everyone was milling around, waiting for the Emperor and Empress to arrive, Prince Odai came to ask me if I had seen the scroll. Prince Odai is only fifteen but he is already an incurable gossip; as soon as Ki, Heguri, and Gorii saw him talking to me they gathered around to hear what he had to say. He told them there was an amusing scroll in the Small Pavilion and made a gesture with his hands which I will not trouble to describe. Of course we all burst out laughing and decided to go over and see it. Prince Odai took it upon himself to be our guide, though we could hardly have got lost following the path around the pond.

Well, certainly nothing but praise can be given for such a magnificent scroll. The marbled grey paper is so thick and heavy that one believes it must be a slab of stone. In fact, there were several arguments about the paper that night, disputes as to whether or not such paper could be made in Yamato. I think it quite goes without saying that such paper could only come from China, but there were several stubborn men, Lord Tabito included, who said they had seen better made right here in Nara. The paper had a red border with silver embroidery depicting waves on the sea. On the matter of the painting itself, at least, there was no argument. No Yamato painter can equal in skill the master of Chang'an who created this scroll. Instead of the same gardens and goldfish and men poling barques beneath willows that one sees so frequently, this scroll depicted a simple room, a tray and wine cups upon the floor, and, upon a bed of robes, a very comely man with reddish hair copulating with a girl. We all laughed, but no one could disregard the simple beauty of the scene: the figures were like two bent stamens at the centre of a flower. Each was so balanced, the man's little hands poised so lightly upon the girl's hips, that it seemed as if there were no force or motion in their lovemaking at all, nor any guilt, for their faces were impassive as Bodhisattvas. Who has known love like this? It was almost saintly, their lovemaking; one had the feeling that the scene was not sordid at all, but rather, sacred.

When Fujiwara arrived, he pushed his way through the crowd of admirers and his face, once he was close enough to make out the details of the figures, showed his surprise. When he turned his head, as a dog will do when it is curious, we all burst out laughing at him.

When we heard the Emperor arrive, everyone rushed back to the Main Pavilion. Later on that afternoon, during the meal, I glanced out at the pond and noticed, on the path by the eastern fence, the grey and pink robes of Fujiwara gliding past the reeds. This I could not resist making known to everyone, that Fujiwara had returned alone for another look at the *Secret Prescriptions of the Bedchamber*. In the midst of great laughter, Tabito bade all the women turn over onto their hands and knees for Fujiwara's return.

I sent him the beginning

I sent him the beginning of the well-known poem:

Come to me, my dearest,
Come in through the bamboo blinds!

but he has not yet responded with the rest. Silly man, could he have forgotten? How is it that he can be so concerned with poetry and yet cannot remember the final lines to such a simple poem as that?

An overheard conversation

Walking past the Morning Assembly Halls, I overheard Tabito and Sakimaro discussing the merits of a book they had both read. I could not see either one of them, for they were behind the wooden partition that conceals the dressing-room, but I recognised their voices well enough and stopped to eavesdrop for a while. Several clerks saw me there with my ear to an interstice in the fence and joined me to benefit from the learned men's conversation. Sakimaro was telling Tabito, in that unmistakable voice that sounds like the soughing of an adze against dry wood: "It was a sordid waste of my time. One shouldn't read such a romance without some perspective on the author's life, so as to see how all events and person-ages are extracted from reality. Do you remember *The Great Voyage*, and how each character's name was an anagram for a real person's? Very fine book, that."

"Tripe!" Tabito bellowed out, very close, and at least one of the clerks with his ear against the wall recoiled in alarm. "You call yourself a Buddhist? Good grief. You, Sakimaro, so certain that you'll be a celebrated falcon in the next life, and you don't believe in imagination? What good is a romance if it's only going to rehash history?"

"You leave out all the humdrum things," soughed the voice of the administrator.

"Then creation is a reductive thing," Tabito concluded for him. "Interesting theory, that one."

I could hear Sakimaro cinch his belt, so starched that it squealed. "Look, what about these poems Yakamochi's been collecting, 'waves of Isé' and such? Would they really be worth reading if you didn't know who wrote them?"

"I don't know anything about them. My son never shows me anything. Whose poems are you talking about? Good grief, is there someone behind the wall?" The clerks bolted. I took a step away just as Tabito delivered a booming kick to the fence. I hurried on my way.

To Otomo Yakamochi

To have loved you who loved me not,
was like going to a great temple,
to bow in adoration,
behind the back of the famished devil.[17]

Things that disgust

Centipedes. Millipedes. Live crabs in a pile. A rough hand at writing. No letter from someone who owes you one. The sound of workmen speaking beyond the walls. White teeth. Curly hair. Coloured nails. More than anything, one's own ignorance.

---

[17] Images of demons were kept in Buddhist temples as a warning to show what state of existence a man might be transmuted to in the after-life through disbelief and evil conduct. To worship these images is, of course, absurd, degrading, and useless. The poem exemplifies Kasa's emotional *volte-face* with respect to Otomo Yakamochi.

A [wo]man's heart

A [wo]man's heart is a shameful thing. When [s]he is with
a [wo]man whom [s]he finds tiresome and distasteful, [s]he
does not show that [s]he dislikes him/her but makes him/her
believe [s]he can count on him/her. Still worse, a [wo]man
who has the reputation of being kind and loving treats a
[wo]man in such a way that [s]he cannot imagine his/her
feelings are anything but sincere. Yet [s]he is untrue to
him/her not only in his/her thoughts but in his/her actions
and his/her words. The [wo]man, of course, has no idea that
[s]he is being maligned.[18]

Hateful things

A seam coming unstitched. Violet or orange in the wrong
season. Carriages that push ahead at a festival and spoil the
view. The *shikkongo shin*. A drop of ink at the end of a very
long letter. A drop of soy on a very expensive silk. Ill virtue in
a beautiful woman. Arriving at Nara Field to watch a match
of *kemari* that was scheduled, only to find that no one is
there. Poor people and the houses they live in and the smell
of their millet boiling as one passes down a narrow lane. One
hears footsteps approaching upon the veranda late at night,
but it turns out to be night service from the Inner Catering
Office or a drunk and wayward guard. Even more hateful
when it turns out to be a gentleman who has come to visit
someone else and one is forced to listen to them all night.
Pickled jelly-fish that have sat too long in the sun. I detest
dried shark. A visitor leaping up first thing in the morning, as

18 Demonstrating clearly that Kasa's pillow book was still in circulation two centuries
later, this entry is identical to one found in *The Pillow Book of Sei Shonagon* (Morris,
p. 144) save for the rebarbative but candid square bracket, which is my addition.

if he had urgent business elsewhere at that hour. An infection that tickles the back of the throat. Liars. Beggars. Nuns. Tonsures. Thin dogs. Soldiers. Commoners thatching themselves like their huts against the snow or rain, walking along Scarlet Phoenix Boulevard like so many piles of mulberry bark and reeking of boiled persimmon juice. The smell of the ditches in the height of summer. Anything that swarms.

Composed on the occasion of my drunkenness

I drank too much last night and my head is throbbing. It makes me acutely aware of her in the corner behind the curtain, plucking her eyebrows and whimpering from the pain.

For the appointment of Otomo

For the appointment of Otomo Yakamochi, new Governor of Etchu Province, a ceremony was held at the Great Supreme Hall. This was the thirteenth day of the seventh month. It should have been an enjoyable occasion, and for many I suppose, it was.

On the first level field are assembled all the lower officials and men of lower rank. Mats have been laid out for them and, because it is hot, there are red parasols for those in the first three rows. In front of these are the eight towering standards of the ministries, their banners and flags brightly dyed — mustard yellow, red, white, green, and black — all stirring languidly in what little breeze there is on the afternoon.

Of course, I watch from far behind, underneath the colonnade. When I first arrive, I am surprised to find that so many ladies have chosen to come to this ceremony; it is very hot and there are other, more elaborate, ceremonies one might have wished to view at another time.

10. *shikkongo shin* ['thunderbolt bearer']
ca. 733, Todai-ji Temple, Nara

We all sit in the shade of the columns and look out across the blinding white gravel of the plaza. Sitting next to me is the Lady Momoé and how tearful she becomes when the ceremony begins![19] Twice I ask her to be silent, but she only shakes her head and covers her eyes with her handkerchief. Yet another of Yakamochi's conquests left in a poetic mood.

I shall never write another poem.

On the terrace, all the high officials come to take their places in front of the hall. Led by the Ministers of Right and

---

[19] *Lady Momoé of Kawachi, to Otomo Yakamochi*

**To this day I have not forgotten
the moon on that pitch-black night,
for my thoughts of you
have known no lull.**

74

Left, they walk up the ramps on opposing sides and file across until they meet at the centre. One spot remains empty in between them. This is the place of the Chamberlain Fujiwara, who dodders over to the spot only after everyone else is already seated. He is an unbearable eyesore, the height of pretence in an already turgid scene. I look around as everyone waits for the old fool to be seated. Behind me, further under the shadows of the gate, there are several attendants, and I can see the silhouette of the Princess Yamaguchi leaning against one of the columns.[20]

I find it strangely enjoyable, sitting here, listening to all the sobbing going on around me, that so many others should be crying when I am not. I feel I will retch when I think of how seriously I believed in our courtship.

When Chamberlain Fujiwara has finally taken his place in the first row upon the terrace, Emperor Shomu appears. His scarlet robes match the parasols and the Chinese columns, yet how tiny he seems. He comes forward, raises his ivory tablet, scatters salt over the stairs and is seated again. Then it is another eternity for Fujiwara to get back to his feet, approach the stairs, make whatever address it is he is supposed to make, and then turn to the assembly and call out Yakamochi's name. Of course, from such a distance I cannot hear anything, but I understand from long experience exactly what is happening. Midway along the third row, one of the red parasols wilts like a single flower in a crowded field. One glimpses Yakamochi then, dressed in yellow, passing through

---

20 *Princess Yamaguchi, to Otomo Yakamochi*

> Not wanting others to see
> that I long over you,
> I find each day troubled
> with half-stirred desires.
> I cannot go on like this.

11. Forecourt of the Great Supreme Hall

the maze of parasols and seated men. He emerges at the right and ascends the ramp onto the terrace. He meets Fujiwara at the centre where they exchange formal greetings, then both turn to face the Emperor, kneeling down before the stairs.

It is at this point, when the Emperor is to confer his decree, that I have had enough. They are all cruel, insistent men, prolonging my torture in the most elaborate and meaningless way. All that ritual is hollow as a locust shell. I go back through the colonnade to my carriage and tell the driver to take me away.

"Where to?" he asks stupidly.

"I don't care. Take me anywhere. Just take me for a drive."

This morning I watched as Koto

This morning I watched as Koto slept. She looked so elegant. How is it she can be so charming asleep and yet so dishevelled and exhausted when she wakes?

Beyond the curtain, the blinds were open on the yard. I saw the Chamberlain Fujiwara approaching from the

Emperor's residence. Fujiwara is elderly and stiff, with long pendulous ears and a jaw bristling with whiskers. He must have very odd knees, I imagine. When he speaks, he uses ancient, obscure colloquialisms such as, "One sardine is better than a mackerel twice cooked", and "Why put two bushels in a one-bushel sack?", and "You can't make *okonomiyaki* without breaking eggs". Most of the time no one has any idea what he is talking about; I myself am convinced he grew up on board a ship.

Fully three-quarters the way along the path he stopped in mid-stride, as if some thought of great importance had just occurred to him. He knit his brow, twisted a finger in one ear, and then turned as abruptly as a soldier and went stalking back again.

How foolish! I simply could not repress a giggle. Hearing it, Fujiwara whirled around and eyed the blind. This, of course, only made me laugh the more. After a moment, he nodded to himself and an insidious smile appeared on one side of his seam of a mouth. He continued on his way.

Splendid old wizard! I have no idea how anyone can be intimidated by him.

The 'morning boy'

There is a young man of the Asagao family who walks past the East Wall just before the second watch every morning. Unless there is some noise interfering, one can hear his voice, a warbling, rhythmic half-chant uttered as he walks up the avenue. I have actually seen him only twice. What I can remember is that his face is quite normal, unlike the distorted features of others that are similarly afflicted by demons. His eyes are always roving, seldom stopping to dwell on any particular thing. Once, last winter, I saw him walking ahead of us through the snow as Princess Takano and I approached the Akatainukai Gate in her carriage. Though it was cold, it was a splendid day for a carriage ride, or a parade, or for some elaborate outdoor ceremony. The odour of the incense that had been burned for our morning ablutions seemed to follow us into the carriage, lingering on our newly washed robes, and coupled with the clear sky and the brightness of the snow and the chanting of the monks from Kofuku-ji filing past... well, I shall not describe it all, but I remember it as clearly as anything. Takano and I sat apart, each to our own shutter and our own thoughts, in a kind of dreamy silence. When we rounded Second Column Road and came up beside the palace walls, I noticed the boy walking ahead of us. Something about his gait held my eye.

Every several steps, as he walked, he made a half-turn to the wall, in the same way that one turns to face someone directly when being introduced. And not only this, but the boy touched the packed-earth wall each time, compulsively. It seemed that had he not touched the wall, that if someone, perhaps, had stayed his hand from doing this, it would have been of grave consequence to him. The rapture in his face, the "aaah, ha! aaah-ha!" he muttered as he walked, the regular touch upon the wall, there was something at once inviting and horrendous about it. The child in me wanted to emulate him. The lady-in-waiting shuddered.

I did not bother to mention the boy to Princess Takano.

On the other occasion that I saw the 'morning boy' pass by the gate, his eyes seized upon the brass rings of the open doors and it was clear that he wanted to touch them. One hand went immediately to his mouth and he hesitated. He stepped closer. He reached out to stroke the shining brass. Then, immediately he had done it, he spun around and went out of the gate, continuing down the east face of the wall.

Now the guards at Akatainukai Gate are rude and cynical, always drunk by night and making ridiculous comments to passers-by during the day. I do not know why anyone suffers them. Still, they left the 'morning boy' in peace. As I think on it, I am inclined to believe that the nature of the boy's 'calling' garners him this respect. His 'duties' are as regimented as anyone's in the palace, and only slightly more ridiculous. No one would think twice about making fun at Lord Tabito's or the Chamberlain Fujiwara's expense, but the 'morning boy' is a model of discipline.

When you left

When you left, you took my composure and my courage with you. I did not know what to do with myself. I should have stayed in one place, but I could not keep still. I wandered aimlessly through Nara, among places so intimately bound to memory that they stung. I wanted desperately to be lost. I kept walking. I passed over a hill and into a valley. I came to a station. I caught the first train to Osaka and lost myself in the crowds.

Later that week we took our bath[21]

Later that week we took our bath together in the morning, Lady Koto and I. Koto is the youngest at court and we all admire her figure. I told her so at the bath but she did not seem pleased.

"I still don't know how to dress as you do," she said.

This, lamentably, is true. Koto receives very poor reviews at court because of a terrible eye for colour. She has made

---

[21] **The Japanese habit of bathing every day had not yet developed. Chinese medical journals of the period recommended one bath every five days.**

several horrible combinations since she came here, and I have had to pull her back into chambers before she makes a fool of herself in company. She tells me then that she hates the court and wants to leave. I daresay she would get her silly wish if I let her dress herself.

Protesting his very good intentions

Protesting his very good intentions, the Chamberlain Fujiwara has taken to visiting Lady Koto in order to "instruct her on proper court etiquette." In theory I suppose this is considered part of his job, but like so many other things it is just not done. Still, there is no arguing with a Chamberlain. So Koto is plagued and it is all I can do to protect the girl from his lechery; she follows me now everywhere I go. Sooner or later, I imagine, she will have to relent to him.

If I were a man

If I were a man I would be attracted to a woman by her figure, not her clothes. But men are shallow. All they care for is a new texture, an elegant ensemble, a brow free of hair, and well-blackened teeth. Is it not the body beneath the clothes that deserves more appreciation?

At sunrise

At sunrise, the Emperor Shomu made his way to the Eastern Precinct Garden and, facing towards Isé Shrine, made obeisance to the heavens, praying to the *kami* and to his ancestors for a prosperous reign and subjugation of all evil spirits. It was a cold morning and, as we stood watching, our breath rose in front of our faces. We gathered our sleeves

melons,[22] and then back to see the Emperor again, never stopping to eat, sleep or even bathe. This morning she got so upset at the Yakushi-ji priests that she told them she would build another, more effective temple.

Lady Koto has been

Lady Koto has been chosen to take part in the Tooth Hardening. This year the ceremony is to be held early, that Emperor Shomu may benefit from its healing auspices. Koto and two other specially appointed virgins will taste various types of spiced wine before presenting them to Emperor Shomu. Radishes, mirror-shaped rice cakes, melons, snow crabs, and other similarly auspicious foods will then be presented to the Emperor in order to 'harden his teeth' [guarantee his health] during the coming year. In the ensuing banquet, the three virgins always end up drinking a great deal and are pursued by the gentlemen of the court. This is why the ceremony is sometimes referred to as, simply, the 'hardening'.

The day she was notified of her appointment, Koto came to me in tears, completely in the dark about what was expected of her. The veranda had been empty. Mount Ikoma brooded purple on the horizon beneath an empty white sky. Closer at hand, three crows watched over the yard from the roof of the Empress's Domicile. I had decided that today I would remain seated, facing the west, until the sun went down. Such lengthy inactivity allowed me to witness the incredible composure of the landscape, so much in contrast to the turmoil in my own life. "Why me why me why me!" Koto pleaded,

---

[22] Although their use in prophesying the future has diminished considerably over the years, melons are still highly valued in Japan. A single cantaloupe costs the equivalent of 30 to 100 American dollars in a Japanese supermarket. The record price paid at auction for a cantaloupe deemed 'perfect' in sweetness, shape, colour, and scent was $1500, bought for a wedding gift. One hopes it boded well.

flailing her sleeves about and completely shattering the day's repose. I sighed. Coming back from very far away, I tried to take an interest in the teary-eyed creature kneeling before me. She was a little red beet pulled from the ground too early, not at all the willful girl I knew she could be. "Why me, Kasa?"

It was, of course, more than likely that Fujiwara, once again, had a hand in her election. I explained this mystery to her in the simplest terms possible: "Fujiwara finds you attractive in more than a friendly way. Or perhaps less than a friendly way. Either way, for him to introduce Lady Koto to adulthood is a fine anecdote, but it's a matter of prestige when Lady Koto is a Tooth Hardening Maiden." Poor Koto looked positively horrified. "Now," I continued, sounding very matter-of-fact even to myself, as if these things had never been new to me once, "the only way to make him lose interest would be for someone to beat him to the prize. The problem is, who would dare to do it? You may be pretty, but stealing from a Fujiwara [or an Ogawa for that matter] would be suicide."

Koto let forth something between a sigh and a moan. "Couldn't we spread a rumour?"

I laughed at the naïve suggestion. "Easiest thing in the world," I replied, "but you still have to fail the examination."

"Examination!" she whispered, her face draining of colour. "What kind of examination?"

How frightful! It was absurd to be sitting there discussing the problem of the girl's virginity with such gravity when in a month's time, or two months, or however long it took before she came to her senses, we would be laughing about it. "Do I really have to explain it to you?" I asked. "Look, just find some young guard or other and seduce him. The clerks from the Saké Bureau make easy prey. So long as you don't have any compunction about ruining a man's career, you'll fail the test and Fujiwara will lose all interest.... Believe me. I speak from experience."

Koto stared down at the mat with her fine little hands clenched pink as flower buds. "And what if I'm already in love with someone?"

"Well then, I hardly need to explain things, do I?"

She thought a moment, and hesitated, and then shook her head. "It's complicated." I wondered what could possibly be going on in her mind, but she was too timid, then, to open any window into her deepest thoughts. "And there could be complications with a man and I couldn't wait until the right time even if I wanted to."

Such a pleasant evening to be so tormented.

"Can't you help me?"

"*Me*? What can *I* do?"

She shrugged her shoulders. "It's all the same, isn't it? A man... or not."

"What do you mean?"

"Just... something in the bath? You could show me where."

"Enough! Please." I felt itchy all over. "Going through with such a thing can't be nearly as vulgar as talking about it so."

Will I have to demonstrate some compunction if I admit that I assisted the girl in her wish? Feeling the way I did about Fujiwara, how could I not feel for her in that situation?

Flowers

The delicate red petals that form the inner envelope around the camellia's stamens stay sheltered while the outer ones are torn by a wind. When the butterfly comes, it probes about inside. Syringa. Pinks. Water-lilies. Short, brown, pendulous tubers. Chrysanthemums protected by paper hoods; the dew drips from the petals onto the paper, and when the hood is removed, the scent remains there for a souvenir. Lotus leaves, spread out upon the water. Cherry blossoms and plum blossoms, but these are not proper flowers so I will not consider them here. Onion flower, longest lived of all the flowers. Hollyhock, that gives a hot, chafing feeling in summer. Wisteria, much prettier than its namesake.[23]

Just as she said

Just as she said she would, her faith in our ailing Emperor as strong as ever, Empress Komyo has begun construction of a temple. Now, instead of spending her days by the Emperor's bedside, she watches the painfully slow process of the temple's construction and takes part in the blessing of every single timber. Today the Princess and I accompanied her. The climate brought about in the palace by Shomu's illness is dour, and the thought of leaving the palace for a little jaunt was a welcome one. I had little idea of the tedious day we would all end up spending.

The Empress's viewing room is a bungalow propped above the ground on wooden stilts. The Princess and I, along with the Empress's ladies-in-waiting, sat up in this box in two rows, with the Empress seated just in front of the first row, peering down through the bamboo blinds at the construction going on beneath.[24]

As the day wore on, and Komyo's silence and the incessant tinkling of her Buddhist rosaries weighed upon us all, I wished that I had worn something lighter than brocade. I

---

[23] *fuji-hara* ('wisteria field'): an acidulous reference to the Chamberlain Fujiwara.

[24] For a time, I was happy in just such a bungalow, or at least as happy as could be expected of one who had lost everything. Rum La Tondeña and the view of the sea and the women on the beach were anaesthetizing. But I am too infected by the bug of the past for such simple medicine. I need this purge, this paean. I need to prove to you that, though I may be dry, there has always been a bit of the biscuit in me.

grew sleepy. Several of the Empress's ladies-in-waiting, who were forced to endure this torture every day, had actually fallen asleep. It was at once sad and amazing to watch how they could retain their posture and yet be sound asleep. And should Empress Komyo even budge, but straighten a sleeve or put a finger to her brow, they were all as instantly attentive as if they had never taken their eyes from her.

After spending the better part of the day on high, we were finally taken for a tour of the temple construction by the architect. He explained that the ground here was sacred. Not so very long ago, there had been a Shinto shrine on this spot which had burnt down in a fire. Far from making the ground unfit for a Buddhist temple, it only made it more sacred. While the architect spoke, I looked at the clutter which surrounded us. The foundation had already been laid and large pillars were being prepared for erection. I thought that the practical work would be done first and the decorating later, but at the same time that the pillars and beams were being cut to length the more fanciful and detailed work of ornamentation was being done too. Here was a rough-hewn beam integral to the structure of the temple, painstakingly smoothed by a half-naked carpenter from the provinces, and not ten yards away was a master carver from China at work on a whimsical transom of egrets, dragonflies, and picotees. Quite remarkable!

The design of the temple is *imamekashi* in the utmost. "With such an advanced temple built in his honour," the architect was saying, "the august Emperor cannot fail to regain his health."

The Festival of the Weaver Star

No festival is more charming than the Festival of the Weaver Star, when the Emperor and the Court seat themselves in his garden to watch the meeting of the Herdsman and the Weaver. "Because of her love for the Herdsman, [represented by the star Altair] the Weaver [Vega] neglected her work on the clothes for the gods, while the Herdsman neglected his cattle. As a punishment the Emperor of Heaven put the two stars on opposite sides of the Milky Way, decreeing that they should be allowed to meet only once a year, namely, on the seventh of the seventh month, when a company of heavenly magpies forms a bridge that the Weaver can cross to join her lover. The magpies will not make their bridge, however, unless it is a clear night; if it rains, the lovers must wait for another year."[25]

A lady of the court

A lady of the court has been admonished for adultery. How can it be that a woman should forget the old bond of love and form a new one? Hm?

Under Bigamy the law says:

A woman who, having a husband, leaves him for another man shall be liable to penal servitude for one year. The offending man shall, after one hundred lashes, be separated from her.

The Imperial Rescript says:

Righteous husbands and faithful wives shall be accorded benevolence and bounties.

One wonders, though, if righteous husbands, by their righteousness, discourage faithful wives.

The Chamberlain searched

The Chamberlain searched long and hard for the one who had stolen his 'plum'. Sometime during his courtship of Lady

---

25 Morris, Ivan, p. 162n.

Koto, someone else had 'visited' her, or so he assumed, and he was livid with jealousy. Lady Koto, of course, would not say a word. Her insouciance was brilliantly affected and Fujiwara was all the more incensed. "You licentious squid! How could you have let this happen?"

"How could *you* have let this happen?" Koto replied demurely, never taking her eyes from the needlework she always seemed to have at hand when he was around. "If you didn't want it to happen, august Chamberlain, why did you let it?" And there was nothing that Fujiwara could do. When he came to question me, I told him the truth, I had not once seen a man visit her.

Thus, a wall of ambivalence greeted the Chamberlain Fujiwara and, though he brooded, his feeble imagination could not find the crack. When I made his anger known throughout the court, it became an even greater source of embarrassment to him than the initial loss had been. Of course, thereafter, he considered me, who had had no real hand in the affair, the principal architect of his humiliation.

I recall a pilgrimage

I recall a pilgrimage we made to a mountain retreat on the third to last day of the twelfth month. It had not been entirely necessary, this pilgrimage, but I felt that we needed time away from Nara together. She was not entirely agreed, but said she would come, hoping to see the snow, as there was none in Nara at the time. We left, as is the custom for such a pilgrimage, at midnight, and as we were crossing the Horokawa by way of Amagatsuji Ferry the moon was shining brightly on the water.

"Let's swim to the moon," she sang, and it did look as if we really could swim to the moon then, for there was only a slim barrier of dead reeds separating the water and the sky. Behind us, the Imperial City of Nara was quiet in sleep. Only once did we hear the keepers of the clepsydrae calling out the hour. On the far side of the Horokawa we continued on by carriage. We drove up into the hills, rattling into the blue tide of the sky one moment and plunging through wet forests the next. This drive by moonlight was unlike any other I have taken; I could not keep our direction or progress sorted out in my mind. It seemed to me that we were going around in circles until we entered a fog and I lost track of our direction completely. Spectres of road signs and wayside shacks reared up before us. I found it quite frightening, but she seemed totally unafraid of the unpredictable darkness and was in the best of spirits. Truly she seemed to thrive when she was away from home. When we finally reached the temple and saw that the sky was lightening above us, and the demure lanterns of the approach were limned against the morning mist, I was very much surprised that we had reached our destination after all. The car stopped and we climbed the stairs to the balcony of the temple. Far below, the road we had taken wound down through the hills and then made straight across patchwork rice paddies and stippled bamboo groves to the collection of dewy roofs shining in the distance that was Nara. The head monk came to greet us there and gave us special slippers. The moment we arrived in our cell, we promptly fell asleep in each other's arms, the last time we ever did so.

In the afternoon the head monk awoke us and we shuffled after him into the sacred confines of Buddha Hall. It was a busy time for pilgrimage and the corridors of the temple were crowded with people. It can be uncomfortable to be among such a throng. The boys charged with conducting our devotions and the monks whom we had hired to say our prayers for us were very helpful and did a good job of clearing the way. The best thing, as anyone with any experience visiting temples knows, is to be preceded by some person of quality down a corridor; that way the commoners have already been cleared ahead of you.

We passed the days with our devotions and watching the other visitors arrive and depart. On the third day we were asked by the head monk to stay awake the whole night as a measure of devotion. I was not enthusiastic about the idea of listening to the monks snoring all night, but we amused ourselves with our own invention and the night was passed without tedium. We devised elaborate personalities for the characters of the old tales and wrote hilarious letters to one another in their hands. I was giggling over an absurd poem I had written in the style of Tabito when I noticed that she was watching me.

"What is it?" I asked.

"I wish we could stay here," she said, pensively. "Or anywhere away. Anywhere but Nara."

"Anywhere *but* Nara? Whatever for?"

"So I wouldn't be so bored. It could be just you and me, and no routines or rituals. It would all be new. With every new place it would be all new again."

"You're reading from a Hemingway story," I told her. "Where would our living come from?" The voice of common sense.

"Damn the 'living', Leo! Your idea of living isn't living at all. Perhaps if you actually lived in Nara with me it would be alright, but you're not even there. You're underneath it. You only see what's lying under the ground. If I had a dollar for every time you pointed out what *used* to be I'd.... I'd buy a ticket back to the States."

"You're being unrealistic. Anyone would think that Nara wasn't the centre of your life."

"It's exactly why Nara is the centre of my life that I'm so unhappy. I'd rather live like a nun than a lady-in-waiting. I'm a *lady-in-waiting*."

I tried to placate her. "We'll go on pilgrimage again if you like." She only shook her head. It was already the fourth quarter and the candle began losing out to the light coming from the shutters. It looked as if she had gone back to sleep, so I set about writing a letter, as I often like to in the early morning. When Koto opened her eyes and saw me writing, she asked me if it was to Yakamochi. I did not bother to reply, for she knew very well that it would be addressed to no one else.

"How is it you can forgive him so much?" she said suddenly.

"Forgive him?" I wondered aloud, looking up from the page. "Forgive him what? What are you talking about?"

She lowered her head. "Nothing," she replied. "Perhaps I'll go see if... " And without finishing her sentence she got up and left.

Such a strange girl!

Later that day we left the temple. I was in great spirits, looking forward to seeing by daylight the frightening route we had taken by night. The thought of returning to the comfortable schedule of the palace made me happy, but in front of Koto, who so detested going back, I tried to conceal my good humour.

The white cat

The white cat of Asaka's, or is it Asaka's at all? The white cat comes around the corner from the Empress's domicile. It stops and its eyes widen at the commotion of soccer in the yard.[26] It is somewhat startled, and unsure whether to continue into the

---

[26] Actually kemari, an ancient game very similar to modern-day Association Football.

open. Halted there, it smells the veranda post, as if the certainty of the scent of urine will becalm it and encourage sound decision. When I look up again from the page, the cat has disappeared. So it is as always, I sacrifice one for the other.

On the morning of the seventh

On the morning of the seventh day I woke to warm pressure along my back and thighs. I thought I knew what the sensation was, or rather, who was responsible for it, but I was surprised because I did not remember going to sleep with anyone. It was cold in the room and I submitted to the comfortable assumption that it was him.

When I woke again I had turned in my sleep. It was not Otomo at all, but Koto. I crawled behind the curtain of state to cry.

Today we showed our best

Today we showed our best *karaginu* for the Observance of the Egrets. We all looked very comely arranged beside the Sahogawa river. Everyone's manners were very delicate for the occasion, and I had the impression that Nara was like a family, for the most part indifferent, sometimes disjunct, but at rare times enjoying this peaceable accord.

This was the day chosen to watch egrets, yet there was not an egret to be found anywhere. We saw sparrows and *hototoguisu*, several geese, a kingfisher, but not one egret. As the day wore on, the novelty of our situation wore off. We began to get impatient. The Bureau of Ceremonies had assumed that this would be the most perfunctory of ceremonies. We would all simply go down to the Sahogawa, spot an egret, and return home where a banquet awaited us. No arrangements had been made for an extended stay. So there we stood, everyone searching the reeds and the sky for an egret.

When we had waited three full calls of the tower, and the sound of the running water was having a predictable, uncomfortable effect upon the ladies, the men from the Board of Ceremonies finally decided to set off to the palace for seats and food and saké and one of those tasteless, but necessary, curtains of state designed for indiscretions out of doors. All the ladies had grown irritable by this time and frowned at one another and the men and the empty river and the indifferent sky. And still there were no egrets.

The situation hardly improved when a column of valets arrived from the palace with mats and food. In our best *karaginu* it was just as uncomfortable sitting as standing. Even the men looked thoroughly unhappy with their lot, stuck outside in formal wear, waiting for a ridiculous bird to arrive. And what good was lunch either, when no one could eat it for fear of spilling? Most of us only chewed on some of the dried shark that was there. Only Lady Koto dared to eat one of the large white peaches that sat in an uninjured pyramid among the dinner boxes. How can I put into writing the envy, admiration, and contempt I felt, watching her sucking at that dangerously dripping fruit?

After still another call of the tower, and the sun high overhead, Chamberlain Fujiwara, losing to his innate irritability the battle to maintain a satisfied air, sidled over to the Minister of Ceremonies and had some words with him. Then he turned to address the whole company. It was only in keeping, said he, with the character of the egret that he not appear before an audience. "The egret is in all things modest and prudent, and demonstrates in his own way the prurience we all wish to emulate."

There was a moment of silence among the crowd, then

several titters from those who understood what he had said. Koto looked at me questioningly as I giggled behind both hands, but I could only shake my head. I would explain later. The Chamberlain, of course, had no idea of his slip and believed that his decision to terminate the ritual was the sole source of everyone's good humour.

Caught in a traffic jam[27]

For the trip to Yakushi-ji temple from the palace I took the ox-drawn carriage of Lord Hirotsugu. Even though no one can see inside, it is a privilege to ride in Lord Hirotsugu's carriage. Only the Emperor's and Empress's carriages are more impressive. Indeed, just as in a royal carriage, one must climb a sort of stairway to enter it, and once ensconced inside the passengers ride high above the surrounding carriages.

We exited through Scarlet Phoenix Gate and started down First Row Avenue, past the university and Lord Yasumaro's mansion, but we got only as far west as Fourth Column Road before we were stopped in traffic. As I learned later on, Lady Aoi had just finished her dedication of the new Lotus Sutra and all the carriages returning from her mansion were turning at that very intersection where the carriages on their way to Yakushi-ji were passing. Somehow they had got interlocked, ox to groaning ox, wheel to axle, and the attendants were crying out at one another to give way, each driver unwilling to move backward as a matter of personal pride. Those behind only tried to push through at the edges, whereupon they met up ox-nose to ox-nose with other carriages

---

[27] In Kasa's time there were sometimes as many as 300 carriages in the main avenues of the city; often they were stuck in massive traffic jams. *Karuma arasoi* ('road rage') was common during processions and other ceremonial occasions when people struggled to get their carriages into advantageous positions. Full blown brawls between attendants and outriders were not infrequent.

14. Scarlet Phoenix Gate

coming in the opposite direction. Some of those caught several rows back then attempted to turn around in order to take another street. This, of course, only locked the carriages even more firmly together, putting several knots in what was already a tangled rope. The shouting increased to a clamour. Several smaller, hand-drawn carriages managed to squeeze past on the left and right, but the more prestigious carriages were far too wide and would have put a wheel in the ditch. By now, there were commoners gathering to watch the commotion at the intersection and their intrusions into the problem only made matters worse.

What a wait we were in for! We knew it the moment we got stopped. Usually such traffic is cause to be upset, especially when it is hot and all one can think of is the shady garden one has left behind and the bamboo grove around the temple to which one is proceeding. But Lord Hirotsugu's carriage is sumptuous and the dominating view turns everything into a spectacle. Looking forward through the lattice window we could see across the thatched roofs of the other carriages right up to the tumult of the intersection. I myself have been caught several times at the very crux of the impasse and it can be a most frightful scene: the attendants, ignoring the orders of their betters, all leaping from their carriages to beat one another with ox-whips and sticks. But in the sanctuary of the Hirotsugu carriage I was quite amused to observe the fighting from afar.

Lady Hirotsugu is courteous and soft-mannered and her husband is unorthodox as only a member of a branch of the Fujiwara family can afford to be. One of his stranger notions was to equip his carriage with a hinged panel in the roof; what he calls a 'moon-window'. Stuck in this traffic jam, he was much desirous of opening the panel to see the commotion from still higher up. Of course, neither Lady Hirotsugu nor I would be induced to put our heads through the roof, so Lord Hirotsugu remained there for the duration, standing up straight in the centre of the carriage with his head and headdress out the roof, conversing with his driver, directing obscenities at the other drivers, and updating us occasionally on any developments in the situation.

Lady Hirotsugu took the opportunity to ask me about Otomo Yakamochi. I had been asked about him by several other women, and to each one I had always replied that I had broken with him, but that he still wrote me every week asking for my forgiveness. To Lady Hirotsugu, curious as a child is curious, which is to say, without premeditation or intent, I told the truth:

"I let him go to Etchu without saying goodbye. I haven't heard a word since." I worried the hem of my over-robe. "I would like to think that he cannot put his regret into words."

Lady Hirotsugu smiled sympathetically. "Do you still believe in him?" she asked me.

"I believe in believing in him," I replied.

She regarded the rosary in her hands. I thought that there was something sad about the way she looked at it, but it cleared and she smiled. "Well, Kasa, he will not be the first man to be saved by a woman's devotion," and she swung the rosary at Lord Hirotsugu's knees.

I was sorry when Lord Hirotsugu returned from his spot in the clouds to tell us that we would soon be on the move. All around us the men were climbing down from their perches on the carriage wheels to take up their positions on the step-boards, others streamed past from the centre of the action, and we saw several of the wounded carried past and laid on the other side of the ditch.

"How delightful!" he cried once he had replaced the panel in the roof. "Soon everyone will have a scenic Hirotsugu moon-window!"

I remember

I remember the time you came through the garden in the rain with a poem that you had written. You had left your notebook out and the rain had ruined it. I said it was not important, you could write me another or recopy it. But you disagreed. You said it was more poetic that I take this one, washed out as it was. I said it looked like an inkblot. You told me it looked like a watercolour. I'm sorry, I don't remember what I did with it.

Time

I can hear the keeper of the clepsydrae calling out the hour. Time is measured only in the capital. Etchu is as far off as heaven.

I saw Lady Sakanoé's Elder Daughter

I saw Lady Sakanoé's Elder Daughter in the State Halls Compound today. I wanted to stop and talk to her, to see how she would respond, but when she saw me she hurried past with barely a nod of acknowledgement. Only as much as I expected.

To Otomo Yakamochi

A moment of silence
grows prickly with questions.
Was I such a bore
that you had to choose others?

To Otomo Yakamochi

One may die from longing, too.
Like the hidden current
in Minase River,
unperceived, I grow thinner
with each day.

Naniwa

In place of the Emperor, who is far too ill, Lord Tabito went to Naniwa to see off the envoys for China and to bestow upon them the Sword of State. When he returned he came to see the Princess Takano and me and he told us about the trip.

"From the windy height of Mount Ikoma," he told us, "there are fabulous views of the Nara Valley on one side, and Naniwa on the other. On the Naniwa side, one looks down over the Yodogawa river and feels great repose. The delta, as most deltas are, is very wide and flat and that noble river

15. Naniwa, Osaka today.

spreads in wavering lines of silver across the fields. In the distance the estuaries flare onto the white tapestry of the Inland Sea.

"By midday one is approaching the town. The first things one sees are the Embassies of Scilla and China, which have fallen into disrepair, and then comes the old palace, hardly in better shape. Beyond the clutter of shacks and shops crowding onto the road is a forest of masts. There are many ships in the harbour, anchored amidst a sea of green reeds. When the ships arrive or depart they appear to be sailing across a vast field of grass. When the fishermen pole their craft out to the open water, one sees no boat beneath them. There were a great many people congregated there when I arrived.

"It was just like a festival," Tabito told us. "Isn't it odd how a perilous sea voyage can make people so happy? You would think China were nothing more than a festival going on just across the Yodo."

Tabito presented the Sword of State to the Ambassador and they had taken the ceremonial cups together. Usually these cups are left empty, but Tabito insisted it was his duty as the Emperor's proxy to drink them full. Then he smeared the crab's eyes with salt and read a poem.

Composed on the occasion of the Embassy to China

From time immemorial,
it has been said that the
Land of Yamato is a gods-given land
where the word-soul brings weal
and the *Kami* reign.

You humble men,
obedient to the sovereign's dread command,
set out this day from
windy, wave-bright Naniwa.

Until you return,
I will sweep the shores of Mitsu Beach
with a washerwoman's besom.
I will wait in a fisher-maid's shack
sipping oft-diluted dregs of saké,
saving the best for your return.
I will climb the fragrant pines
of Mitsu and watch
the black, wind-woven sea
for your return.

I can hear the fisher-maids
in their tiny boats
rowing out to sea —
Lying in my fisher-maid's bed
I shall hear the sound of your oars.

When the Ambassador boarded and the three ships finally eased away, several people crowded onto the docks tumbled into the water. Tabito and his men had to push back the crowd in order not to fall in themselves. They watched as the vessels were carried slowly south by the current, across the meadows of reeds. When they reached the open sea, and their masts had diminished by the distance, the sails unfurled like three small white flowers on the horizon, one after the other, in perfect succession. A cheer went up in the crowd.

"At that moment," Tabito recounted, "I felt the most profound unease, as if I had been out there on those white waves myself."

"That's not unusual after eleven cups of saké," said Princess Takano, a quip which we both took great delight in.

"Bah!" Tabito laughed. "It wasn't that. It was the endlessness of the delta, and the windswept sea, and the mountains of Awaji, and the tiny ships... it gave me shudders. Naniwa felt to me like the beginning of the end of the world. Where could one go after Nara? There is no *after* Nara. Nara will be the capital forever, the one and only capital, and you can hang me from a ridgepole and I won't change my mind."

Coffee[28]

Much ceremony is made of taking coffee in the mornings. By the sound of their bell we know the five men who serve the coffee are coming. They dress in red robes and matching silk hats and they come very slowly along the verandas for they are all blind. Only blind men are chosen to serve coffee, as no one in the palace is suitably dressed to receive in the early morning. The man who leads the way holds the bell

[28] Tea was not introduced until the ninth century, and even then was considered a purely medicinal beverage.

and the one behind him carries the mill. Two men are needed to carry the large pan of coals upon which sits the water
pot, and the last man carries the bowls. Once they have
mounted the veranda and started serving at the first partition, the scent of the coffee carries and everyone gets very
anxious for them to arrive, always peeking out of doors, listening for the sound of the berries crackling in the mill. If
one has a lover visiting he will often postpone his departure
when he hears them coming.

They must know the palace better than anyone, these
men. The man with the bell slides the door open for the rest,
never searching for the door seam at all but reaching out with
perfect confidence, as if he can see exactly what he is doing.
The other men follow him in by the sound of his feet.

The coffee-men are greatly respected in the palace and all
hold rank. I rarely drink coffee myself. I simply enjoy watching the ceremony. Should I ever have to leave Nara, I will
miss this morning ritual as much as anything.

I harbour a secret intention

I harbour a secret intention that this pillow book will
reach beyond my cloistered world.

Now the illness

Now the illness of Emperor Shomu seems more serious
than anyone had thought. There are many kinds of sickness
and I wonder if even the Bureau of Astrology are certain what
is the matter. This morning they placed several large
manekineko at the door to the Emperor's apartment in the
hopes that good spirits will be welcomed inside. Certainly
there is a shortage of good spirits now. The palace is a quiet,

16. *manekineko*

eerie place. No one practises music. The royals do not go to Nara Hill for hunting or for sport. When the snow falls, there are no snow mountains built and it melts where it is in the warmth of the afternoon sun. I saw Prince Asaka looking under the verandas for his white cat, but one of the nurses came to find him and bring him back indoors. Even the coffee-men bring no joy in the morning. Gone are their little jokes, making believe they can see one's burly knees or compromising state of dress. Now their doleful file through the yard reminds one only of a funeral procession. I see Lady Awatame taking her coffee upon the veranda across the yard. She cups the steaming bowl to her face and stares across the opposite roofs to the white morning sky and the ever-changing Mount Ikoma, now lying very flat on the horizon.[29]

---

29 *The Maiden Awatame, to Otomo Yakamochi*

> Is there no way
> For us to meet again?
> Next time I shall hold you with sorcery
> to my white cloth sleeves.

Normally, she would not take her coffee outdoors in the chill of the first month, but the palace is quiet and we two are the only people out. I too stare to the north-west, past Mount Ikoma, but in my mind I am seeing the Province of Etchu.

To Otomo Yakamochi

Strong rooted, like the sedge
on the base of the rocks
in the Nara Mountains,
are the feelings we bound our hearts with.
I cannot forget.[30]

That very afternoon Fujiwara

That very afternoon Fujiwara came to our Domicile with a retinue of Imperial Guards. He quite rudely opened one of the doors without first calling and took several paces into the room. Through the interstice of a curtain of state I saw him peering over the bamboo screens trying to find someone. "You must all come to the Emperor's quarters," he called out to the ceilings. "You needn't ask why because I myself have no idea. Just put on your best robes and some make-up — you especially, Gorii, and don't keep me waiting."

---

[30] We met in these very mountains, if you will deign to remember, although the sedge was not of great interest to me then. What had my curiosity piqued was bird stool. I was poking with the nib of my pencil through that of a recently departed rook when a blonde woman came along the path. You hello-ed, passed by, but could not resist asking. I explained my interest in seed dispersion. I was advancing an hypothesis that certain plants were brought to Japan much earlier than believed by wayward or migratory birds. Those? Oh those are bits of crab shell. Rooks are notorious scavengers. Our feathered friend must have found the paradisal alley behind some seafood restaurant. Many places, I suppose. Nara is my home. Six years. Vacationing, are you?
  Seven years later, it turns out that you were.

"Emperor Shomu?" I stuttered, totally confused, my head still pounding from the night before.

"Well, who do you think?" he barked. "Who is that? Is that you Kasa, you silly creature?" He stalked back out the door. "Bad enough that he ask for all of you, but to send *me* on the errand...." Hardly a minute went past before I heard him stamp in again. "Are you ready yet? What do you mean, keeping the Emperor waiting?"

Fujiwara would tell us nothing and we only learned later on that everyone in the palace was to be summoned to pray at Shomu's bedside. So we were all alarmed, and all quite literally shaking when we arrived at the Imperial Apartment, completely in the dark as to why we had been called there. My own knees and elbows were clammy with perspiration and I could not catch my breath as I stood before the entrance. The brass doors opened inwards into darkness and noise and the smoke of thousands of sticks of incense burning. Through the murk I could see many Chinese screens arranged to form a corridor down the centre of the room. All along this corridor were the Emperor's Imperial Guard spaced at intervals of several feet, all of them twanging their bow-strings to ward off evil spirits. Behind them, I could see the gallery, several rows of high officials and women of the Fujiwara family who peered through gaps between the screens and whispered to one another incessantly. At the end of the corridor, in a haze of smoke, were doctors and diviners, all huddled around the Emperor's bed. The Chamberlain Fujiwara preceded us down the corridor of guards, stopping four times to kneel down and pray along the way. Each time as I knelt down I looked to left and right, and felt a great many eyes upon me. The twanging of the bowstrings surrounded me and I had a vision then of a lonely traveller on a dark path who hears, in the moment before he is struck down, the soft, evil chorus of bows in the trees around him.

When finally we had reached the end, the cluster of men in robes and Chinese caps parted, and I could see through the haze the form of the august Emperor lying upon a kind of dais surrounded by cushions. He was lying on his side covered by a green robe and several tablets with mantras written out upon them had been laid across his body. At the head of the bed was a screen depicting bone-white egrets stalking pink crayfish in waters of nacre. One of the men nearby leaned over him: "The Ladies in attendance to your daughter, Lord," he whispered.

The Emperor's eyes opened and he stared around him wildly, as if he had come back from very far away. The tablets clattered to the ground, and though I was frightened to death I felt like crying for him, who looked so frightened. His is the kindest of faces, the Emperor's, but in that moment of uncertainty it was the saddest and most confused. He blinked several times and, seeing the semi-circle of doctors around him, became calm.

He coughed and turned his head to look at us. When he spoke, his voice was gravelly and hoarse. "Well, Kasa, Ki... Gorii," he coughed again, "un-mis-ta-kable as ever. You've come to pray for me have you? You know I've been having visions all this time, sleeping and awake. I'd like for someone to write them down. What a wonderful thing to have a book of dreams. But I can so seldom find the energy to recount them." He took a deep breath, and clearly limned against the sheet were the bones of his torso. "Such a pity," he continued, suddenly tired again, "all wasted. I shall probably recover fully and not remember a single thing."

He seemed to think about this for some time, staring straight ahead, until his eyelids once again began to flutter and sink — opened suddenly with the same wild fear that subsided to fatigue in its turn, the eyelids fluttering, closing, a butterfly contemplating flight and deciding better.

"Time for you to go," whispered the Chief Diviner. "He must sleep well while it is light.

We followed him as he dropped to his knees and retreated down the corridor. The circle of robes clustered around the Emperor shut like a cabinet door.

Once we were back outside the sun was blinding, and I had the feeling of waking up from a nightmare. I almost stumbled from the veranda and several Imperial Guards were called upon to lead us back.

I was held in thrall

I was held in thrall that moment when she entered the bath, the first time together. She was doubled up, her breasts against her thighs and her fingers poised on the tiles, caught between the cold air and the water's scalding heat.

Prince Asaka's cats

There are kittens everywhere now that Mumyo has given birth. Princess Takano, who is not at all fond of the filthy creatures, has ordered that they be taken to live in the East Palace and that they be kept there by the Inner Catering Office. Prince Asaka was greatly angered by this. He likes to play with the kittens very much, and though I was not sorry to see them go, I did feel sorry for the feelings of the little prince.

When I saw him his face was very round and red, and he marched through the yard in his robes like an angry little cabinet minister.

I called to him. "What's the matter with Asaka-chan today?"

He glared at the blind a moment before he walked over, pushed the blind aside and climbed in. He sat down right across the brazier from me and put his hands upon his knees.

I am always charmed by the way children enter a room. There can be the most solemn or secret ceremony taking place and they will walk right in and pipe up about whatever concerns them.

"Takano-chan's got rid of the kittens," he told me unhappily. He knotted his fingers and would not look up.

"Oh really?" I replied innocently. "What did she do with them?"

Asaka seemed not to have heard me. "There were *seven*," he said, "and the orange one was the eighth."

I nodded solemnly.

Then Asaka's face brightened a little. "Why don't you ask for a kitten, Kasa?" he asked. "The woman from the *kofun*[31] said she would take one."

"We'll see, Asaka-chan," I replied. "Kittens require a great deal of care."

He looked at me skeptically.

"What woman from the *kofun* anyway?"

"The woman from the *kofun*," he replied in an inexplicable burst of laughter. "There's only one woman from the *kofun*!"

This I found perplexing. The *kofun* were ancient, overgrown tombs. I had never heard of anyone coming from there. "Asaka-chan, what does this woman look like?"

"She's tall." He looked away from me and toyed with some excelsior that was on the floor next to the brazier. "And she wears white."

I stared at the boy in wonder. Had he seen the same

---

31 'tumulus' — Just north of the Nara Palace Site are several keyhole-shaped tombs surrounded by large, deep moats. They are evidence of early Yamato rulers, so the name *Kofun* (360–710) is given to the period preceding Nara.

woman I had seen that night? Had he actually spoken to her? Then a thought struck me and I almost laughed out loud at my own gullibility. "But that was Lady Nakatomi, wasn't it, Asaka-chan? She's not from the *kofun*. She got married to the Rector at the State Halls, don't you remember? She asked you if you would like to be married someday too."

The child frowned. "Not *her*," he said. "The woman from the *kofun*. She was here last night while everyone was drinking. She said she would take one of the kittens to live in the *kofun* and I could come visit."

I must have looked quite perplexed at that moment. Asaka frowned and scrambled to his feet. He picked up a handful of the wooden shavings and marched away, tumbling them from one hand to the other. At the end of the veranda he shrieked and hurled the shavings into the air.

Later on, I learned that he had told the same story to several others, including Princess Takano. She came to find me and ask what it was all about.

"Asaka-chan's been telling me all kinds of frightful stories about a woman in a white robe who wants to take one of his cats. Just who is this woman from the *kofun*, anyway?"

To comfort the Princess, I tried to make light of Asaka's odd story. "Next week he'll meet a unicorn on Nara Hill," I told her. "He's just making up stories."

"Perhaps." She put a finger to her lips and bobbled back and forth on her heels as she always does when she does not understand something. "It's troubling," she said. "Perhaps we'll keep a close eye on Asaka-chan for a while."

In Ancient China

In ancient China, the Emperor Taitsung of Wei prohibited the use of saké, but those who continued to drink it in secret referred to white saké as 'wise man' and pure saké as 'sage'.[32]

To Otomo Yakamochi

I dyed my dress
with the violet grass
that grows on the field of Tsukuma,
but before I could wear it,
its colours were exposed and faded.

To Otomo Yakamochi

In the loneliness of my heart,
I feel as if I should perish
Like the snow
Upon the pines in the long, long afternoon.

A letter

I was writing a poem yesterday afternoon on the east veranda. It was a pleasant day, as nice as I have seen in this month, though nothing to compare with the rich, windy days of autumn. When Koto passed by, coming from the luncheon thrown for the monk Dokyo, a favourite of Takano's lately, she saw me and asked what it was I was writing. It was nothing of any importance, I replied. She stopped and stood there watching me from the stone path.

"I don't believe it," she blurted. "You said you would never write him another poem."

---

[32] In ancient Japan, saké was not as strong as it is nowadays, probably averaging between 7 and 10% alcohol. But due to a number of factors, not least of which was the absence of fats from the Japanese diet, it was extremely intoxicating.

This was embarrassing.

I began to fold the delicate white paper.

"Show me it," Koto demanded. I continued folding. "You're afraid to show me. I can see your hand shaking." Swiftly she came onto the veranda as I tried to slip the letter into my sleeve. "You'll just wrinkle it, so you may as well show me," she cried, grabbing me by the forearm. "Kasa, show me!" Her hands twisted at my wrists and I cried out in pain. I wrenched my arms away and crawled frantically across the floor, the letter still crumpled in my hands.

"You would have shown me if it had been for anyone else," she whimpered.

I straightened my over-robe. "And what of it? What can you possibly know, you child?" I demanded, panting. "So he's been seeing other women, you tell me? So he's going to marry Sakanoé's Elder Daughter? What has that got to do with his love for me?"

"That's pathetic."

"No," I argued, "what is pathetic is losing my devotion to a rumour."

"Rumour!" she laughed, getting to her feet. "It's common knowledge! How could it not be, with every woman in the palace pining for him?"

"And does that 'every' include you?"

She stared at me. "Are you so blind, Kasa?" With that, she brushed her robes of dust and went down the veranda. When she came to the end, the lining of her robes flashed yellow as she stepped into the sunlight.

When the Chief Diviner

When the Chief Diviner arrived in the doorway he carried with him his ivory tablet and a melon. No one had expected him to choose to use a melon, and furious whispering like the sound of wind in tree branches could be heard up and down the room. In such a grave case, a diviner tends to turn to a more reliable and prestigious method of augury, for instance, roasting a tortoise shell upon an open fire and reading the future by the cracks. What with the killing of the tortoise, the knife inserted under the shell and slid swiftly around to separate it from the body, the rich blood streaming down the blade, and then the loud cracking of the shell in the fire, all this provides for a much more drawn-out spectacle than the simple slaying of a melon. But the Chief Diviner chose to read a melon and his decision was much criticized. In discussion with the other ladies later on, however, I found myself defending the choice. Sometimes I suspect the motive of a priest who continually chooses tortoise shells and looks down upon melons. The Chief Diviner's decision revealed his contempt for spectacle and his concern for accurate prediction, regardless of the tastes of his audience.

In any case, the melon was placed upon a wooden block, and without any ado the Chief Diviner brought a hammer down swiftly upon it. It squelched and broke each way into several chunks connected by a smattering of seeds and juice and orange flesh. Everyone jumped. Now we all expected, myself included, that the Chief Diviner would spend a great deal of time examining the results of his hammer-blow and picking over the seeds and chunks of fruit to divine their meaning, but no sooner had he smashed the melon than he dropped the hammer and cried out, clapping his hands with delight.

"Good tidings for our Emperor! Good tidings for the Emperor of the Land of Yamato!"

A cheer went up in the room and I was almost trampled as the crowd leapt to their feet and pushed against the line of

Imperial Guards to gain a better view of the melon's carcass. Two Assistant Diviners immediately rushed forward and removed the block of wood with the melon upon it. With the block held between them, they scurried crabwise down the corridor of guards and out the door. Everyone strained overtop of one another to get a look at the melon as it went swiftly past. In a flash I saw Koto in the crowd; her face distracted me from the passing melon and I missed it completely. Once a melon has been deciphered, of course, it is of no more use. The melon was taken immediately to the fire that had been prepared for the expected tortoise shell and pitched directly into the flames. Once the melon is gone, everyone disputes just exactly what he saw, and wishes for just one more chance to see it.

To Otomo Yakamochi

I too shall;
let him not forget.
Let there never be a time
when the winds cease to blow
upon Tananowa Cove.

A fire

A fire destroyed one of the buildings at Kofuku-ji temple. It started in the afternoon and burned through the night. The next morning Princess Takano and the rest of us went over by carriage to see it. During the night we had watched the great tower of smoke, glowing orange by the light of the fire, but in the morning there was only a dismal grey pall over the entire city. We went around by the south in several carriages, past Sarusawanoike Pond and then up the hill. As we came closer, the smoke swept past us and stung our eyes. There was a great chain of men in the trees between the pond and the temple, conveying buckets of water, and they all had cloths tied to their faces.

Closer to the blaze, I watched amazed as the sun beamed into the dense smoke, creating its own architecture of shafts and columns and overhangs, the lines unwaveringly straight against the spinning cataracts of smoke pouring from the eaves. All around us drifted the char, dropping down from the sky among the finer ash. The soft silver paper of moths, millions of them that had been drawn to the fire in the night, lay scattered upon the ground. It was ineffably sad and beautiful. No temple has ever been paid such silent, touching homage.

Everyone back at the palace was very upset. But it really did not matter. All of the important relics and sutras, the soul of the temple, had been taken away for cataloguing several days before.

To Otomo Yakamochi

Pining in my wait for you,
like the pines on Toba Mountain
where the white bird flies,
I have gone on longing
through these months.

A bonze

A bonze came to visit us in the palace today. He was rather short and curiously dressed in black, and his tonsure had begun to grow out. In all, he had a very ramshackle, dishevelled appearance, like a dog afflicted with the mange. He had come to show the Empress Komyo a skull which he had brought from Maizuru that resounded like a bell when struck with a small hammer, but since the Empress was busy worrying over the new temple she would not give him an audience. When Princess Takano saw the man leaving disappointed she took pity on him and invited him to her apartments instead. The bonze was very much pleased by this and immediately came over, holding up the skull on a stick. This object immediately stole our attention. It had a clear shine and 'spoke' with a pleasing, ringing voice. When it chimed, everyone's attention was stolen from the self-conscious remarks of the stuttering monk.

With the monk there had also come an insect collector and a *philosopher*, but they too were ignored. All were engrossed by the skull and hardly paid them any attention at all.

A poem

The fishing fires far away
on the plain of the sea,
Oh make them brighter
that I may see the Land of Yamato.

Several winters ago the supervisor of the East Market

Several winters ago the supervisor of the East Market was appointed to a one-year position in the Dazaifu. Of course, there are few men who relish the thought of leaving the court, especially to go as far as Kyushu, but the positions there are well-paid and the man actually looked happy upon the day of his appointment. He made a great many preparations for his stay, and when he departed he left his holdings in Nara in the charge of three deputies. The senior deputy was responsible for three-fifths the man's merchandise and lands, the middle deputy for three-tenths of the merchandise and lands, and the junior deputy for one-tenth.

When the supervisor returned from the Dazaifu the next spring, he reckoned his accounts with his deputies. The senior deputy rendered him the account books for his year of absence and the man was pleased to find that not only had the rents been raised on all his properties, the sale of foodstuffs had been transferred from the market to direct bartering with the Fujiwaras. In all, his normal income for the period had almost doubled. The middle deputy had much the same in the way of good news. He had bought out the workshops of several competing craftsmen (one of them the Chinese sculptor who did the transoms for the Empress's temple) from the West Market and had installed them in one workshop in the East Market. Working in unison, the business these craftsmen had begun to generate was several times more profitable than the separate stalls which the middle deputy had originally sold to buy them.

When the junior deputy timidly provided his records for the period, the East Market supervisor was upset. All was as he had left it. There were seven hundred Chinese coins and four stalls in normal operation. The junior deputy could have been sleeping for the past year and he would have made as much profit. Now, at court, such a return would not have merited any punishment, but without any hesitation whatsoever, the East Market supervisor dismissed the junior deputy from his service.

Having lived all his life in the market, the junior deputy, or ex-junior deputy, I should say, left the East Market and, naturally enough, made his way to the West Market. There one may see him today, singing and playing *sho*. Whenever I am down at the East Market, which is not often, I admit, I look for him, and once I dropped a coin upon his mat. He is destitute, certainly, but in a strange way admirable, or as admirable as a commoner may be, for now he does what the others did not do: he makes something out of absolutely nothing. Of the marketplace, he makes a stage, and of the air, music.

Still, if only he had those coins back — this is the thought which must torment him mercilessly.

Calm water

Calm water moves me deeply. The sky is reflected so perfectly that there are two skies, and one sees the Land of Yamato as the *kami* see it, although they are free to pass from one sky to the other as they please. They say that a man who drowns in calm water does not die at all, he only steps through.

The hours past midnight

The hours past midnight are the most dangerous, when evil spirits are abroad and those unwary may be infected. To keep the Emperor awake, the coffee men have been directed to change their hours. They are now making their rounds at two o'clock in the morning. Obviously it makes no difference to them whether they serve by day or night, but for the rest of us it is somewhat upsetting. No one questions this measure of solidarity, but one certainly hopes that Emperor Shomu will recover soon.

On the third day of the eighth month

On the third day of the eighth month was held the Festival of the Golden Trowels, although this year the trowels were all made of silver, as every available ounce of gold has been used in the gilding of the *Daibutsu*. A small coffret filled with coins, virtu, and *mokkan* granting various favours is buried somewhere within the palace grounds. The Bureau of Divination and the Confucian University, working harmoniously together, develop seven series of seven riddles each, for a total of forty-nine riddles. The solution of each riddle is the location of the next, except in the case of the seventh riddle, whose solution is the location of the coffret itself. There are seven teams, counting four members each, drawn from the seven pre-eminent families of Nara. Each team starts with one riddle. When a new riddle is found, the old one must be deposited in its place, in order for the Bureau of Divination and the University to verify later on that the progression of solutions was not influenced by chance. This is an important rule, as there have been cases in the past when a team, entirely by accident, has stumbled upon a riddle further advanced in the sequence, or one from another series and, whether by ignorance or treachery, have taken it as the riddle for which they were looking. Each member of the team, I hardly need to point out, carries a golden trowel with which to excavate the prize. No shovels are allowed, for a shovel is a brute instrument and could easily damage the coffret as it is being unearthed.

The morning of the hunt, in a ceremony at the State Halls, the Emperor bestows upon all teams in search of riddles the right to enter any office, abode, or enclosure on the palace grounds. The only places off limits are the Emperor's own apartment and the melon garden. This right of entry leads to a great deal of damage being done by the more inept teams, who come foraging through one's room or garden searching for riddles which are not there. Last year, the Fujiwara team all but destroyed Pebble Beach and the young cryptomerias planted around it in the belief that they had correctly interpreted 'I long for Mitsu Beach', when of course, considering the ideogram used, the reference was to a pine tree somewhere or other. After the teams are given permission of entry, it is time for the caching of the riddles and of the coffret itself. The team members are blindfolded and everyone assembled in the State Halls must face the south until the doctors and scholars have returned. I always feel sorry for these men, for, having returned from hiding the forty-nine riddles and burying the coffret, they are sent to a field beside the Horokawa river in Amagatsuji for the duration of the hunt. Possessed of the locations, they are not allowed to remain in the palace for the hunt itself and thus can never witness the ruckus of the search, the teams cheered onward by parades of onlookers, or the jubilation of the winning team at the final discovery. The doctors and scholars are only allowed to return once the search is complete, in order to verify the win. I remember once when it took two full days to find the coffret. The palace was in a state of chaos, and we were all very glad when the Sakimaro team finally solved their series of riddles and uncovered the coffret beneath the floor of the Imperial Catering Office. The poor doctors and scholars, stuck outdoors on the banks of the Horokawa river for two days, came back looking very sunburned and haggard.

This year, the day of the hunt dawned clear and warm... but this is just another anecdote of my invention and I wonder if I haven't already related enough of them.

I dream of your return

I dream of your return and go over each detail of that day with the greatest of precision. I get up on the morning and go about my toilet. It is spring so I am wearing many layers of scarlet and forest-green under-robes and an over-robe of transparent, lustrous fern. I dress very carefully, making sure that each layer reveals the one beneath it at the hem. I knot my hair in a Chinese mirror, pluck out my eyebrows and pencil in new ones, blacken my teeth. Just dressing takes two calls of the watch or more, for I savour every detail and set it perfectly in my imagination, like a stone fitted into a Chinese mosaic.

The coffee arrives and breaks my train of thought. I fill the cup to the brim from the bottle of Tondeña beneath the chair, imbibe carefully because it is still hot, set the cup down on the boards of the veranda — this endless veranda! Most people have a nostalgic appreciation for verandas, but this one positively drums with the footsteps of my past. Staring ahead, it stretches to a great distance at either side, and all the ghosts of my past congregate in the peripheral crush.

Things that are beautiful

Evening is falling. An ant-borne shred of philodendron leaf mimics the sail of a yacht, shudders as it crosses the frets of sand. The seagulls turn orange as they wheel in the last of the sun. Music drifts from a yacht at anchor. These things are beautiful... but only momentarily. Dwelling on them for too long allows memory to seep in and tinge their attraction with melancholy. In Japan, beauty has always gone hand in hand with melancholy. Even here I cannot seem to break from tradition.

To Otomo Yakamochi

Distant are the grassy plains of Manu
in Land's End;
men say you can conjure them
in your heart, and yet —

On the fourth night of the first month the Emperor dedicates a light to the Deity of the North Star. Tapers are lit in honour of the Great Bear and a banquet is held during which young men and women dance and disport themselves.[33] This year, the festivities started off uncommonly sombre; Emperor Shomu's condition had worsened in recent days and no one was in the mood for levity. The banquet would not have gone on at all had not Shomu, ever mindful of the importance of the calendar, even in his illness, insisted that it take place. Though no one felt like celebrating, there was no choice but to do as he said.

The night of the banquet was cold and stars hung in garlands above the Land of Yamato. Yet this placid sky had no inkling of the tumult that was to take place in Nara that night. The banquet started at the East Precinct Garden and everyone clustered into groups beside the fire boxes. Quiet and pensive, they drank even more than usual, and very soon the supplies of saké in the Main Pavilion had run out. A group of gentlemen decided they would escape the dour scene by going to the Saké Bureau to find more. Once they were gone, Koto came to find me where I was seated before that door which overlooks the 'Healer' Stone. She kneeled down quietly beside me and stayed there, tearing off fibrous strips of dried shark from a wide slice and holding them next to the brazier to soften them before folding them into her mouth. A fire box sent the crooked silhouette of the 'Healer' swaying to and fro across the water. When Koto had finished snacking on the shark, she put her hands between her knees and sighed. "It's cold," she said with a slight pout. As they always

---

[33] These dances later evolved into orgies and were abolished, after which only the innocuous, but guiltless, lighting of the tapers remained.

are on days of a festival, regardless of the weather, the doors of the pavilion were wide open. "Kasa?"

"Yes, Koto?"

"Will you come with me up to the Saké Bureau to get warm?"

Now Koto had been avoiding me since she had caught me writing the letter. This had suited me well, for Fujiwara was still in a temper and interrogating her daily. The less he saw of us together, the less reason he had for any suspicions. Koto's suggestion was a fine change of heart and I agreed. I was content that such a small gesture might at least put us on friendly terms once again, and it was unlikely that the Chamberlain would go up to the Saké Bureau with the rest. When we arrived at the Saké Bureau there was already quite a crowd present, but we found a vacant stretch of bench, actually an empty water conduit leading in from the well outside, and sat down on its edge. Still somewhat awkward around one another, we drank a little more than was necessary for our good humour. In the warmth and sweet aroma of the Saké Bureau I was inclined to be gentle with Koto. She could be charming when she wished, not the indifferent or churlish or weepy Koto, but composed and affable.

All around us were courtiers and ladies seated on wine casks, rice bales, and troughs. In the centre of the room, a drum of saké had been unlidded and one of the bureau's clerks was busy filling proffered bowls with a ladle. Indeed, there was a chain of bowls going around the room like the bucket parade that day when Kofuku-ji was on fire. Some musicians were playing in one dim corner, *koto* and *sho*. Every now and again among the murmuring and the sighs someone would break into a moan, a kind of drunken dirge for the ailing Emperor. The Inspector-General Uamakai was one among several who dropped to their knees on the floor and composed sad, impromptu poems for Emperor Shomu: "*How incensed was our Emperor, that day we courtiers of a hundred clans went out to sport in Saho Vale, leaving the palace unattended! Confined within the palace for thirty days punishment, how we yearned for the heady fields of spring! Now that I remember it, how dear was Shomu to us even then, like a stern father!*"

It was deeply moving to hear a man so carried away by grief. I could not help but shed tears. Soon the lamentations grew louder and the moaning turned to wailing. A strident competition began among the courtiers, each one trying to better the others in the outpouring of emotion. At first they used only their voices, but when Prince Yuhara leapt up with his sword drawn the mourning turned violent. He rushed into the centre of the room with both hands gripping the sword's hilt, strewing drunken tears from his inflamed cheeks, and crying out wildly. His red eyes seized on the cask of saké from which the servant was still ladling dutifully and he stepped up to it, crying out: "*With the bounteous wine the doughty warrior blesses, striking at it with the point of tempered steel, Drunk am I now — I!*" He brought his blade down with both hands upon the clerk's ladle, narrowly missing the man's hand. The ladle shattered into the barrel and the clerk jumped back with a scream.

Everyone was instantly on their feet. The tensions of the drunk found sudden release. Violence burst upon us without hesitation. In the rush to find shelter, I remember seeing Junihito strike out at a wall of stacked barrels with his foot. It folded in slowly at the centre and collapsed around him, whereupon others danced forward through the clutter and pinioned the rope-knotted barrels on their swords or sent them hurtling across the room. Those struck by the flying shards of wood or doused in wine instantly lashed back with

126

fists and feet and sword-hilts and *mokkan* and barrels and *sho* and the paddles used for stirring the young saké that snapped with a loud crack. There seemed no exit from the mêlée that erupted around us, and we ran here and we ran there to seek refuge, but the whole building was a foreign landscape to us, like a jungle in battle, bears roaring, tigers leaping, women screaming, men crying out in pain. I backed into the wall, my heart tied up in my over-robe. I felt like laughing at the impossible suddenness of it all and yet my eyes were streaming with frightened tears. I truly believe I would have been crushed by a barrel had not Koto stepped into the water conduit and pulled me behind her. Where the conduit disappeared through the wall, we ducked through the access and found ourselves stumbling across the grounds in the darkness. From outside, the bureau resounded like a drum with the commotion. Men rushed past us from the gate, flooding towards the centre of the action like jubilant moths to a fire.

It was only the next day I learned that the bureau had actually been destroyed during the brawl that ensued, the stocks of barrels and straw set on fire by a smashed oil-lamp.

With unusual presence of mind, Koto led me away from the riotous scene and up past the sleepy Sewing Bureau. Instead of turning into the Imperial Domicile, however, she turned to the right, making for Akatainukai Gate.

"Where are we going?" I panted, trailing behind her breathless pace.

"I don't know. Why don't we go outside the palace? Have you ever seen the moon from Nara Hill?"

I hadn't, and for good reason. "It's not safe, Koto. There are footpads beyond the walls. And the hairy Ainu."

This she found quite humourous. "How silly you are sometimes, Kasa. There's no one out there. At the moment, we're actually safer outside the walls than in them." Judging from the din still resounding from the Saké Bureau, she may have been right. As it turned out, Akatainukai Gate was unmanned; all the guards had probably passed us on their way to the fight. It was no trouble, then, to open the small inset door within the gate and, without quite realizing the gravity of what we were doing, I followed Koto through.

The sandy street where I found myself was bounded on one side by the packed-earth walls of the palace and on the other by the mansion walls and bamboo fences that marked the eastern edge of the city. To our right, the moon lit up an uneven plane of rooftops sloping gradually down to the Sahogawa. Koto turned to the north and we walked in the wheel ruts where there were fewer stones to worry our feet, the sound of our slippers on the sand inordinately loud in the silence. The wall on our left soon met up with First Row North Avenue. Beyond this were the woods surrounding the *kofun.*

"Shall we go in?" Koto asked me when we had come to the crossroad.

She was crazy, I whispered. Nothing whatsoever would induce me to go into the woods around the *kofun* by night.

"*Kofun* nothing," she retorted brazenly. "Let's go see the moonlight on the moat." And with that she crossed the avenue and disappeared into the trees. "Aren't you coming?" she called back.

"Koto!" I hissed. "Koto, come back here!"

Only the crepitating of her footsteps through the fallen leaves remained, and these receded quickly until they were indistinct from the thousand tiny sounds of the night. I approached the edge of the road. Between the trees, the white thread of a path stuttered through the moon-shadows. Koto's ghostly figure glowed luminescent in the moonlight before it disappeared among the trees. I stepped carefully through the brush and followed the path after her.

"*Koto!*" I stumbled over roots and stones as I followed but felt little pain, the soles of my feet already numbed by the gravel of the road. My heart echoed in my ears and I could feel the chill of sweat below my neck and across my breasts. I crossed meadows and tripped through copse after copse until, suddenly, out of the shadows before me, shone a tenuous web of silver filaments hovering in the air. I took it for a spider's web, but my out-thrust arms found nothing there. This web, as if I had frightened it, seemed to retreat, slightly trembling in the moonlight, giving way at its centre to recede outward in concentric rings that slowly disappeared into the trees around me. I stared at the fabulous apparition until it was gone. Then there came a low, uncertain sound and a new web erupted into view, propagating outward from its core as the other had done. If only our understanding could focus on reality as quickly as our eyes. The wall of perspective abruptly gave way and I found myself staring at the reflection of moonlight upon agitated water. It was the moat of the *kofun*.

"Over here." I followed the voice down to the banks of the moat. "Are you alright?" She was standing next to the shore, looking across the water. She tossed another stone into the centre of another spider's web. Of course, only now as I recreate it can I appreciate the beauty of the scene. At the time I was so furious with Koto that, 'the moon shone red' upon the water. "You... irresponsible..." I seethed, still afraid to raise my voice in the stillness. "Why did you run away?"

"You wouldn't have come," she replied simply.

"Of *course* I wouldn't have come. This is no place to be in the middle of the night!"

It struck me that she was wearing no jacket, and that her top-knot was undone, her hair draped straight in front of her.

She tossed another stone.

"You've lost your jacket?"

"I suppose."

"Do you suppose you might have lost your mind too?"

"If only you knew why," she replied intriguingly, turning to look at me.

"Tell me why then, Koto," I replied impatiently. "Tell me why so we can go home."

She took her time, felt the ground around her feet for more stones. "I understand that you still love her," she said, then changed her mind. "No, that's wrong. I don't understand it. But at least I acknowledge it now."

"Very well. That's very good, Koto. I'm pleased at your personal revelation. Now, shall we go back? You're going to freeze."

She went on as if she had not heard me. "I don't understand why you love her in particular, she's so old and ugly, but that's just personal preference, I guess." She came up from the water's edge and put out her hands. This was not the plastic skirt-wearing teen I had known (yes, in *that* sense of the word) that afternoon on Mount Ikoma. That was a college girl on a dare, seducing her professor for a lark and then calling her friends from the next room on her cellular telephone. This creature before me now was inquiring, sensitive, sensible even. Her hands found my wrists and slid up to the elbows, her thumbs pressing into the hollows. I could smell the sweet, stale saké on her breath. The things she said were so forward that I cannot let my pen repeat them, they would glare in the darkness like neon. When she spoke, it seemed to me that, as with all things sentimental, there had been some crucial development left out. But the development was in Koto's own mind. Physical intimacy had assumed, in some convoluted way, a corresponding emotional one. She had been dreaming of this moment for weeks, watching it in her mind like landfall in a sailor's, until it had gained all the weight of reality, and so she never thought of questioning it. To her, there was nothing out of place at all in confessing her love for me, not after the hours of premeditation that she had devoted to it.

I was terror-stricken. It was as if you were standing just across the silvery water there, instead of across the Pacific, staring at me, and I should certainly drown trying to reach you, to protest. *You* left *me*! This situation is not my fault!

I undid the buttons of my inverness and stepped forward to wrap it around the shivering girl. Her petite, girlish torso nestled into the fabric that smelled of me. "No," I said, the first one for her, the rest to steel myself, muttering, knocking my fist upon my forehead. "No, no, no, no, no...."

She loosened her grip on the cloak. And hiccuped. "Why can't you leave her behind? She's *gone*! She's not coming back."

I can't. I can't, Marilyn.

The girl pulled away from me, shrugged the cloak from her shoulders, and threw it into the moat. It lay there a moment, unfolding languidly until the fabric succumbed at the edges and began to sink. (There, it's finally gone. I shall never find another tartan like it. I hope you're pleased.) We were both rather stunned to see what she had done. But she reacted first. I stared at the water, my cloak out of reach, and listened to her scramble back up the path.

Sounds of water

The chuckling of the stony stream in the North Palace Garden is lovely, but one cannot help thinking of the servants working to keep it running. Through the interstices of the fence, one can see them ferrying buckets from the canal, flickering back and forth like ghosts while the bright, gay banquet goes on here. The crackling of water falling from the eaves in the fifth month. A curtain falls into a trough between the flat, black stones. It is always a disappointment to pick one of these gems up and see how, as it dries, it becomes just another common stone. After the first week of rain one no longer hears it. The screaming of children when the downpour starts. The twanging of the guards' bowstrings during a thunderstorm. Rain upon the roof. Tiles are most dramatic, especially when they fill an empty hall with their moaning. Thatch is too demure and cedar shingles sound too hollow. The best is the drumming of the tiles in the State Halls. The plashing of hands. Silence.

What had seemed to me

What had seemed to me a straight course from the road to the *kofun* turned out to be a network of deer trails through a hundred unfamiliar woods. I tried to make my way by the moon but there was never one path which led in the direction I wished to go. I could hardly draw a breath I was so frightened, and this whole landscape, cruel and cold, seemed to have cropped up from the evil seeds of my momentary weakness and Koto's misdirected affections. I felt at once the traitor and the betrayed. I was forced to take a hundred detours, each time hoping that the trail would swing around and lead to the road. But none did. I was lost in the forest north of the city all night, wandering through the trees only in my white under-robes and shivering with the cold. Finally I could stumble no further and I collapsed in a small clearing to await the dawn. I can hardly say if I slept then, it seemed that sleep crept around me, came over me by turns, and I would come to with a fright, forever unsure of where I was. Sometime during those hours of mixed consciousness I felt the gentle, cold touch of snowflakes upon my bare arms and face.

When the sky began to lighten, and the close, opaque shadows of the forest slowly retreated, the flat darkness giving way to a welcome but dismally grey perspective, I got up from the ground. Through the trees I could see Nara lying on the plain below in a rigorous grid, the melting streets standing out sharply against the white rooftops. I would have appreciated such a view from the warmth and comfort of a carriage, but I was cold and in no mood to dally. Only in retrospect can I appreciate the scene. I made my way down from Nara Hill. I no longer worried about following the helter-skelter paths, but picked my way through the undergrowth until I emerged at the site of Todai-ji Temple. Protected by the roof of thatch, the thighs of the *Daibutsu* were barely dusted with the snow, two small hills of bronze in the middle of a landscape that had turned white. It was still the early morning when I followed First Row North Avenue down to the city walls. I was hoping that Akatainukai Gate would still be unmanned, but the small door had been locked and I was forced to sound the bell. A small window in the gate opened and there followed the rudest of interrogations from a bearded face that appeared there. You're not Kasa. Kasa's a pretty one. A temporary lapse. Let me in.

As I made my way down past the Sewing Bureau and the smoking remains of the Saké Bureau, I witnessed the destruction that had been wrought the previous night. All around me was the detritus of the fighting and the fire. There were smashed barrels and swords and *mokkan* scattered across the street, robes, rinds of pork fat, headdresses, shoes, an inkstone, tapers, and broken vessels of all kinds. The smell of smoke and boiled saké drifted over everything. I entered the Imperial Domicile at the nearest point to my room, hoping there would be no one awake to witness my humiliating return; I could only imagine the rumours that would sprout from such an entrance. From the gate to my own apartment I followed the stone path past the azaleas and naked hedges around the south end of Takano's apartment. Two figures stood on the veranda. For a moment I thought I could turn and go back without being noticed but, just then, Koto's head turned and her guilt was laid bare in her eyes.

"Well, well," said the Chamberlain Fujiwara, for it was his narrow figure standing there beside Koto's. "The morning nets all sorts of strange fish."

I advanced warily. "I apologize for being out, Chamberlain. I was at the Saké Bureau when a fight started and Koto and I —"

"Now, now," he broke in with a magnanimous tone. "You needn't explain anything. Koto has done a detailed job of it already." Koto would not look up from her feet. "It was all very mixed up last night, wasn't it, Koto?" He put his arm around her waist. "I am sure the Lady Kasa did not mean to waylay you."

"But one does wonder," he continued, now addressing me, "about your intentions, Kasa. I did, in fact, guess that you were responsible for my embarrassment regarding the Tooth Hardening, but it was the least plausible of my ideas and I really only fantasized about it. I had no idea that you could be so — no. Shhh." He put his index finger to his lips, his brow wrinkling with anger and disbelief. He came down the stairs towards me. "What was it that proxied for the Chamberlain Fujiwara? Some *bath article?* It *is* devious, Kasa. Intriguing but devious."

I wanted to scold Koto for going to him, for succumbing to her childish side instead of accepting my feelings like an adult. But I could not speak out. The Chamberlain Fujiwara was in his element. He put his hands behind his back and loomed before me. He smelled the air. "Hm. Lovely morning. There must be a good tide down at Naniwa. Well, now you must hurry home. I'll make sure the coffee-men come to visit you first."

"Koto — " I tried.

"No.... Shhh. It's morning, Kasa. Be at peace. Please. I said go home."

I shook my head as impatient tears came and I rushed past him down the yard.

To Otomo Yakamochi

Longing for you
leaves me helpless with despair.
I lean against a little pine[34]
on Nara Hill, grieving.

In the late afternoon

In the late afternoon, I was resting in my apartment when a courier came to summon me to the State Halls. He carried, wrapped in yellow silk, one of the elegant *mokkan* of the Emperor's Office. I had seen such a package many times when Princess Takano received them, but I had never once had one addressed to me, and at first I thought the courier was lost. Unfortunately, he was not. We went down to the State Halls together, past the Imperial Compound gates, through the Imperial Domicile, and into the State Halls Compound by that small single door at the rear of the compound walls that has always looked so mysterious. I had never

---

[34] One of the very rare instances of a translatable pun, common to both English and Old Japanese.

come this way, and I was amazed that the courier should be so at ease passing through the very sanctuaries of the capital. We passed down a gravel walk between two log storage houses, the roof of the Great Supreme Hall towering before us. Before we reached its shadow, we turned up a flight of stairs into the North Wing and after some confusion of corridors, passed through a door and found ourselves in the sanctuary of the Great Hall itself. All around and above me loomed the shadows, though I was blinded. The doors along the west wall were open and the last orange sunlight flooded across the floor, shining like brocade woven with grey where the column-shadows crossed it. The sun was setting over Mount Ikoma.

I turned to face the dais at the front, but at first all I could see was an orange disc still hovering before me. When finally the glare melted into the depths of the hall, I made out the Chamberlain Fujiwara and the Ministers of Left and of Right seated cross-legged upon the dais. A figure was kneeling before them in apparent supplication. Though I could not see her downcast face, when I kneeled beside her I could tell that Koto had been crying.

The three men were dressed, respectively, in the usual tricolor of judicial robes: grey, white, and black. When I came closer, I saw that their headdresses were of the hard silk variety, and even as Fujiwara began to speak I was preoccupied by their ridiculous appearance: they began with a black leather band at the forehead; then, higher up, there followed a kind of embroidered sack over which the peak, splayed with whalebone, towered like a huge black spoon. All this was secured by a large red rope knotted conspicuously above the left ear, the tassels dangling onto the shoulder.

The Minister of Left was a heavy-set and ponderous man, cut from stone, though the whalebone in his headdress must have softened over time, for the 'spoon' was as curled as an

Indian's thumbnail. As for the squat little Minister of Right, he was deep asleep, his spoon slowly dipping and rising in motion with his breathing. The Chamberlain Fujiwara, at centre, was the most intimidating of the three, simply for his rigid posture, although when he spoke he revealed himself for the malicious fop he has always been. He seemed to be in a state of some excitement, his eyes alight, glancing about the room, rubbing his knees, cracking his finger joints.

"Welcome, welcome. I am glad we finally get to converse in a more formal setting. I find conversation with you somewhat trying when it isn't guided by policy, Kasa." He cleared his throat with a grumble and a rough spate of coughing ensued. The Minister of Right woke just long enough to smile at all present and nod away again. "Ahem. Let's cut to the bone, shall we? Lady Koto has just confessed once again to the ingenious method by which you 'engineered' to make her fail the examination for the Tooth Hardening. I am glad for the Minister of the Right that he slept through the gory details of her admission." The spoon rose and fell, the snoring peaked and subsided, as if the Minister of Right were a sleeping demon in a tale. "Now I will not deny," continued the Chamberlain, examining his tumid knuckles, "that I had a certain interest in her participation. Indeed, any man as robust as I would have felt the same inclination. But we must not overlook the fact that the Tooth Hardening is crucial to the Emperor's health. That there was one less maiden than usual this year has had a disastrous effect upon him, may the *kami* forgive me. And who is to blame?" His hands spread questioningly then slid back together, his long fingers woven into a complex ball that he held in front of him. "With respect to Lady Koto, I fail to see in your actions anything less than spiritual treason, Kasa, perhaps even statutory treason." Compressing chins, his cronies nodded in agreement, one intentionally, the other by coincidence. "Does this make sense to you? Are you following the drift?"

Koto's sobbing increased.

"There we have it. One can see the compunction in Lady Koto's spirit. It, at least, has not yet hardened into a barnacle. Considering her lack of experience, we have decided to be lenient in her case. She has been offered the chance to redeem herself by a life of virtue at Isé Shrine." At this point I felt as if I would retch. "She has gratefully accepted. But we have doubts, Kasa, that we may expect the same repentance of you in such a place. Indeed, after leading Lady Koto astray, what kind of havoc would you wreak in a community of nuns? Ha! Hrrgh," and he began coughing again, barking at the ceiling like a dog.

I took the opportunity to speak. "Princess Takano will vouch for me," I called out loud, my eyes on the floor. "She believes in my intentions."

"Hcch. Ehem. On that assumption you may be mistaken. Oh, here they come. We've ordered a little meal. Please, you are invited as well."

Incredulous, I peered back at several valets from the Inner Catering Office entering the hall from the giant doors. They brought fruit trays and lacquer dinner boxes and jugs of saké to the front and set them up on the dais. As if he had been faking his sleep, the Minister of Right opened his eyes at the very moment a bowl of drink was placed before him, and without moving his head, his 'spoon' still horizontal before him, reached out and sipped noisily at the cup. A small, elegant dinner box was set before me as well. It was one painted with a pattern reserved for the Imperial Family. To have eaten from it on a regular day would have made me faint at heart.

"Please, please," the Chamberlain prompted. "The crab is fine this time of year." I remembered staring at the

Emperor's coffret one day, long ago, when I had first arrived at Court. Everything in between was a dream. "Oh, come, come, Kasa. I have to obtain the approval of Emperor Shomu to get my claws on you, and for that we'll have to wait, may the *kami* look well upon him. We'll send you home to your parents for the time being. You should find it most relaxing."

Under the pretext

Under the pretext of monthly defilement I was sent to my parents' home just beyond Amagatsuji Bridge. They were very surprised to see me when I arrived at the door, for they had no idea of my predicament. They rushed about in the way that worried parents have, preparing my room with a new mat and hanging paper plum blossoms around the door. Only once evening had come and there was nothing left to do did they dare to ask what the meaning was of my coming home. Had I come to tell them that I should be married? Had I received an appointment of some sort? *Had something gone awry at the palace?* Don't be silly, it's just for a change. It's only the monthly defilement, only the monthly defilement. It's nothing at all.

This morning, when I opened the screens onto the garden, the sun was shining very brightly and the little bamboo, wet with dew, shone even as brightly as those of the palace.

To Otomo Yakamochi

Not even in my dreams
did I imagine it:
that I would be returning
once again
to my native village.

A messenger came from the court. He handed father a letter and asked him to read it aloud. Father turned to my mother, standing behind him in the hall, and his face had blanched white as a radish. I can only guess that he assumed I had been disgraced in some way or other and that this was the letter expelling me from Court. He swore to my mother that he could not read it. Understandably, this annoyed the messenger very much. He took his *mokkan* from his sash and smacked father on the shoulder with it, telling him to do his duty. But father could not.

"Whatever my daughter may have done, Lord, please forgive her."

Of course, the messenger was extremely embarrassed to be addressed as 'Lord'. Red and indignant, he snatched the letter back from my father's hands, tore the ribbon from it, and unfurled it in front of him.

The first half of it was full of a great many ritual prefixes, after each of which father moaned in agony. I could not understand the import of these passages, or, rather, made no effort to understand them, because I was breathless and dizzy and the sight of my mother and father weeping was too much to bear. Yet in the end, when the messenger finally reached the text of the thing, it was only a letter from Lord Tabito, informing my family that he was coming for a visit. "Please be vigilant in attending me," it read. "I shall be tired and thirsty from the ride."

Father stared with eyes wide as soy saucers at the disdainful messenger. "Lord Tabito? Lord Tabito is coming here? Lord Tabito?" He whirled around and embraced my mother. "Lord Tabito!" Bursting with happiness and pride, he turned to the messenger and tried to take his hands in gratitude, but the messenger stepped away from him and refused to stay another minute in our house. He rolled the letter up again, deposited it on the chest near the door, and strode out. Father followed close behind, making offers of all sorts of gifts, but the man would have none of it, and quickly rode away.

It was later the same afternoon that Lord Tabito arrived. Once he was done with the visiting formalities he begged a moment alone with me, and we left the house by the rear gate and followed the riverbank west. The Sahogawa was low and the grasses which rustled in the chill wind were still their fulvous brown of winter. On the opposite bank, only several yards across, groves of bamboo creaked and groaned, sharp cracks echoing as the tall spires clashed in the wind. Beyond the bamboo, the Nara Plain stretched far to the south and a gentle charcoal line above the horizon was the only indication that these flatlands led to the mountains of Wakayama. After a long while spent thinking, holding me in insufferable suspense, Tabito sighed and pushed the soft *eboshi* back on his head. He asked if what he had heard was true.

Mount Ikoma swayed as the inevitable tears welled in my eyes. "She came to me for advice," I explained. "That was all. I was shocked at what she proposed, Tabito, but how could I not feel for her?"

"You assisted her then."

"I pointed things out."

"So." He rubbed his tired eyes. "It hardly matters anyway. Fujiwara wants the full extent of the law brought against you. He wants to tie you to a crab post to put it bluntly."

"A crab post?"

"Don't ask. I don't want to frighten you," he said. "What did you ever do to old Fujiwara to make him so upset?"

I replied: "I was in Koto's position once."

His chaotic white eyebrows arched. "So that's it. You, ah... didn't use the same method —"

"No, a clerk from the Saké Bureau."

There were many egrets here looking for prey in the shallow water. Beyond another copse of bamboo upstream, we could see the bridge at Amagatsuji. Tabito took his thumbs from his belt and crossed his arms decisively. "Kasa, I think I *do* want to frighten you. Just so you understand how serious this is. Do you remember when I told you about going down to Naniwa? All across the reed sea there are wooden posts driven into the seabed. At night the crab fishermen hang fire baskets on them and the crabs come to the light. The fisherman simply waits for them to cluster around the pole and then plucks them up with a net. Fujiwara wants to tie you to one, so the tide will come in just up to your neck."

It seemed too far-fetched to believe. Until now, writing it down, I had formed no image in my mind of what Tabito was describing. Thankfully, he did not give me the chance to dwell on it. "I'm going to intercede for you, Kasa. I'm going to send you to my friend Moroé, down in Kyushu. Yes, that pig. But that pig likes you. And pigs are honest, not perverse."

I shuddered. I would never go.

"You used a mere clerk to escape Fujiwara before," Tabito argued. "You shouldn't mind using a Governor General this time."

What convenient logic! It was just like a man.

"So be it then," he snapped. "That's what I am. I'm not going to give you a choice in this." His voice hardened. "I'm sending you to Naniwa after dark. You will tell your parents that you are going on pilgrimage. You can reasonably expect that this is the last day you will spend within sight of Nara."

We walked back home in silence. He led me in through the gate and then, before entering the house, stopped and

17. Mount Ikoma, my last afternoon in Nara

turned to me once again.

"By the way, were you really dressed only in white that morning?"

"I gave my over-robe to Koto," I replied. "She was cold."

He nodded. "Very well. It doesn't matter. Princess Takano was just curious."

To Otomo Yakamochi

Not knowing
I am in Uchimi Village,
where they pound their sleeves
on the fulling block,
he does not come to see me,
though I wait for him.

Where the egrets

Where the egrets stalk the clear, shallow waters of the Sahogawa live many crayfish. The young are pale pink, almost white, and the older ones are coppery red. The children here catch them by an ingenious method. They attach a piece of dried squid to the end of a length of thread. Facing the sun, their shadows thrown away from the water, they dangle the bait on the sandy bottom and wait for a crayfish to amble over and grasp it with a claw. Once the crayfish has hold of this savoury treat he will not let go of it for anything. The child, then, has only to pull gently on the string, lifting the crayfish from his element, dangling by one claw in mid-air. Then the child shakes the crayfish onto the grass and taunts it to snap twigs or watches as it flails, turned over on its back. The crayfish always seem to end up getting crushed in one manner or another, for this is the cruel way of children, who have not yet been taught compassion. So the crayfish is killed by what it craved. There are always many cats waiting to carry away the remains.

I can overhear my parents

I can overhear my parents whispering in the next room. They are overjoyed. They have been paid a call today by the great Lord Tabito of the Imperial Court! When his palm-leaf carriage comes for me tonight they will be thrilled. The light falters; a draught catches the flame and sends the nervous shadow of my brush dancing across the page at triple speed.

The tide was out and many small boats rested on the strand. An elderly fisherman stumped back to the road from his shored-up boat, and his elongated shadow sent a profusion of small ghost crabs scattering across the dark mud and glistening green algae. In stark profile against the pale hills were the bamboo scaffolds where the crab fishermen hung their iron fire baskets by night. The sky was empty except low to the northwest where cloudlets glowed in the late sun like an arc of juggler's oranges.

Crackling across gravel, the carriage began along a row of shops and fishermen's shacks that fronted the estuary we had been following since the morning. Through my small shutter window I inspected this quiet, smelly version of the West Market. The shanties filed past like battle-weary soldiers, their helmets blackened and crumpled, their faces cast down, hawking on the ground before them the bandy collection of trinkets they had collected from poor campaigns. Of course, I have never seen a battle-weary soldier but, all the same, this is how I imagined them.

So this was Naniwa. It was the centre of the bay, though it seemed, in fact, more vulnerable a place than protected. The day was only more expansive and indifferent to look at, this row of fragile hovels cowering beneath the imperious sky, as vulnerable as if they were upon the open sea. I could see now what had so upset Lord Tabito, why he had been so anxious to return to the comfortable folds of the Nara Hills.

Between the shacks pathways led back into a wilderness of chicken coops and vegetable gardens. I often find common people quite charming, especially when they are in the rain, or silhouetted by a sunset, but to see them so close up, stooped over and going about their unimaginable business of survival, made me shiver. They were dressed in garb unbelievably crude and the language they spoke, if it was not the mere barking of dogs, was almost entirely foreign to me. Their presumption, moreover, was truly insulting. Instead of concealing themselves when someone of quality was obviously coming by, they stood about brazenly, gawking at the carriage as if it were that of a Fujiwara!

I find strange pleasure in cringing at these memories, but at the time I was so filled with trepidation that I felt I could vomit. How can I describe the fear I had of being alone among commoners, many *cho* from my home in Nara? And was I to be sent by ship even further away? To the very wilds of Kyushu, or even further? I could not imagine that it would happen. I imagined that the Emperor would vouch for me and I would find myself back in the company of Princess Takano and the Court. I would resume my pillow book with a decent inkstone.

As we continued, the paths widened into alleys that stretched back through row upon row of the same decrepit shanties, an army of beleaguered soldiers. After what seemed like many more *cho*, a prominence of trees and a tiled roof enlivened the view. This, I assumed, was one of the old embassies of Scilla or of China, with windows boarded over, literally tumbling into disrepair. Several alleys later the once great Imperial Palace of Naniwa came into sight, a steep slope of tiles that rose above the jumble of the town like a scree of green talus. The next alley revealed a collection of masts where the harbour lay. We rattled down this lane, so narrow that the sound of the wheels boomed in my ears, and I thought wearily of Scarlet Phoenix [not 'Vermilion Sparrow'] Boulevard. Presently there came the sounds of activity, a great deal of shouting that grew more and more strident and deepened with the groaning of oxen. A mountain of broken saké barrels tumbled into my narrow view and suddenly the port was revealed beyond them. Here the reed plain of the estuaries was replaced by an inky harbour and large black docks, weathered versions of the miniature one giving onto the pond at the East Precinct Garden. The shore dropped at a steep angle to the water and there were fire boxes, very much like those in the gardens of Nara, resting there upon iron stilts. Here were ships larger than I had ever seen: low, wide vessels with their own houses built on top. Evidently they were being prepared to go out with the next morning's tide. Carts and drays were queueing upon the docks as pallets of goods were lowered on pained ropes through holes in the decks. As if we were there merely to offload more cargo, the carriage pulled up to one of the queues.

The beacon height of Mount Ikoma

So many years I had seen that mountain from the other side, watched its personality change like a girl blushing when the sun passed by, downcast and weeping in the storm. From the other side I did not recognise it at all. All that day, as we crossed the sandy islets between estuaries, bridges which remonstrated louder than the carriage itself, Mount Ikoma remained an unforgiving shadow upon the horizon.

I do not know exactly what

I do not know exactly what she told them, but it was a lie suitable to provoke the ire of the entire clan. After stretching the truth to accommodate her childish anger Ms. Ogawa did, at least, demonstrate one twinge of misgiving on the answering machine in my office, informing me in rather blunt terms that, unlike the Fujiwara, violence was sure to be the Ogawa's primary method of persuasion. Now vendetta politics were endemic to Old Iceland and Renaissance Italy, but in the Nara Period there was nothing of the sort. Only with the arrival of the *samurai*, centuries later, did Japanese history devolve into the same interminable series of plots and counter-plots. I find such histories lamentable and dreary and I had no wish to be a part of one. I gave up what was left of my Nara.

How can I help you? Girl at the travel agent's office.

I'd like a ticket.

Where are you travelling to, sir?

I have no idea. Yemen. (Half-hoping she will not believe me.)

I can route you through Mumbai tomorrow.

No. Somewhere today. This morning. Where can I go this morning?

Manila, Honolulu, Guam, São Paulo, Vancouver, San Francisco... Cape Cod, Massachusetts perhaps?

Should I have followed you? Only you will ever know the answer to that question.

The activity on board

The activity on board the ship ceased sometime during the night. The light of the fire boxes played silently upon the flanks of the ship. All that remained was to wait for the tide that would draw the ship down to the Inland Sea. I knew that if I were to avoid spending the rest of my life in Kyushu, never to see Nara again, never to see Otomo again, I would have to leave that carriage and set off on my own. Even with the daunting prospect of the voyage before me, I was loth to leave that comfortable silk box. In the darkness I fingered the tassels above the door and the Chinese cushions and wondered if perhaps it would be the last time that I would be so fortunate as to ride in such a carriage, though I had been used to them my entire life. I tightened my waistcord, gathered my robes in my arms, and crawled out.

It was the first time that I had been outside all day. The cold air of the morning was invigorating, but there was little else of any consolation to me in that sleep-dead town. There was no light in the sky, yet the grey outline of the shack-row was limned against a lighter grey, like a row of Chinese characters written with water. As for the ship, it was entirely concealed in the mist. The last thing I wanted was that the sun come up to find me wandering alone through Naniwa's decrepit streets in twenty-two layers of silk robes. I would be robbed and turned over to the police and put on the back of the first horse to Nara. I wished to put some distance between myself and the harbour, where the driver would soon wake and begin searching for me, so I began to walk in the direction, or so I imagined, of the road which had brought me into Naniwa the day before.[35]

At the third quarter of the third watch

At the third quarter of the third watch, I came to a beach. This, I was certain, was the Mitsu Beach that I had read about. As I followed the shoreline, the road passed through a copse of winter-barren ginkgo trees and emerged facing another estuary of the river, this one wider than the rest, so wide and straight, in fact, that I could see all the way down to

---

[35] It is hard not to be envious of the headstrong Lady Kasa. She is a genuine historical personage of the Nara Period. She acts simply and sincerely, unfettered by the self-doubt which centuries of over-emboldened feudalism was to inflict upon the mindset of the modern age. She, unlike the living, is entitled to a better fate than the mantle of obscurity laid upon her by history.

where the smooth flow of the river met the waves of Naniwa Bay. Here the soil became whitish and dry and the air was filled with the calls of waterfowl. The road merged with a wide beach cabled with creeping fig and dotted with clumps of equisetum, and indeed, before long, I did see above the dunes the trim thatch roofs of the fisher-maids' shacks, more rustic than ramshackle, the windblown grass around them strewn with flowers both cultivated and wild, and bamboo mats of winter-picked persimmons set out to dry in the sun.

Pulled up close to the dunes were small oval boats tied to stakes driven into the sand. Though the sun was not yet up, the women had already returned from fishing. I heard their voices and laughter. I passed piles of white shells and several clay tracks leading back through the bluffs. There was still no sign of the famous pines of Mitsu Beach, but at least the 'fisher-maids in their tiny boats' had turned out to be something more than myth.

In times past

In times past, the twelfth day of the second month was the Festival of the Damsons, but because there are so few damson trees left, there is not much of a ceremony to be had anymore. Most people in the palace do not even know what a damson looks like. I remember one from my childhood which grew just beyond the stile, although even this was a hump-backed old commoner of a tree. Anyway, because of the lack of damsons, the festival was to have been cancelled this year. When Emperor Shomu heard about the plans to skip the festival he was upset. He ordered the priests and Confucian scholars from the Bureau of Ceremonies to his bedside and then lectured them, with all the poise he was capable of mustering in his condition, on the importance of retaining the features of the Shinto calendar. They were not to be dropped out of hand but perpetuated in different forms or melded, if necessary, with new ceremonies from China or events from the Buddhist calendar.

The Confucians complained: "This is a problem, Lord. How can we have a Festival of Damsons when there are no damsons?"

"Damsons or not, the festival goes on." This was the Emperor's final decision.

The Bureau of Ceremonies had great difficulty in deciding upon a suitable substitute for the damsons until one of the priests came upon an innovative solution. So it is that on the morning of the twelfth day of the second month there are no banquets or parades scheduled, there are no costumes to be assembled, no feasts to be prepared, but everyone in the palace goes about his usual activity bearing in mind that whatever he chooses to do, whatever is in his routine for the day, is the ceremony itself. Thus, for a short time, routine and ceremony are one. This leads to a general feeling of good humour among the inhabitants of the palace. It is no longer a penance for the officials to get up with the sun and ready themselves at the Morning Assembly Halls. For the commoner, the rice bale and persimmon basket are not so heavy as usual. The child is undaunted by the prospect of morning lessons. In the eyes of one standing on the beach, this ocean is less an impediment than a medium. One wishes the Festival of the Damsons lasted longer than one opiated day.

From beneath the sands of Mitsu

From beneath the sands of Mitsu a road emerges and leads one away from the shore. Here the air is warm no matter what the season, and the trees are all flowering. The variety of plants one finds is confusing, for there are many that one may not find in Nara at all. The sun rises quickly into the sky. One sheds one's quilted over-robe and carries it rolled into a ball. A tunnel of bamboo provides some respite from the heat, but all too soon one returns to the blaze of sunshine. One has to squint to see, and all one can make out in the glare is a scumbled profusion of plants at either side. The light here is much brighter than at Mitsu Beach, where the dew still hangs upon the dune grass. As the eyes grow accustomed to the sunshine, one sees that one is on a path onto which broad-leaf plants cascade, heavy with the weight of flowers and small red fruits.

One has the feeling that the carriage, the windy beach, the dim, sleeping, slapping harbour, are all part of a distant dream.

Like the fence around the North Palace garden, concealing from view the servants who make the stream flow bucket by bucket, the thick trees at either side of the pathway obscure all but the occasional flash of a wide vista beyond. Many more sandy pathways diverge from the main one.

A boy emerges from the foliage.

He is dark-skinned, dressed only in rose pants and green sandals. One thinks he must have come just recently from the bath. He seems to take an interest in the personage before him, as can only be expected the way one is dressed, in a veritable mountain of brocade. He scratches his neck in momentary indecision and then sets off down the path. Without knowing exactly why, one continues behind him through a maze of gardens. Very soon we arrive at a clearing.

At the opposite side is a small hut on stilts. It is somewhat like those of Naniwa village, constructed of bamboo and thatch, but instead of a small crude opening in front, the hut is surrounded by a veranda. The blinds are up. Upon a sort of laid back chair, there sits a red-haired man dressed in white trousers. He is writing with a small brush upon a tablet of yellow paper that he holds propped against his bare, powerful chest (burned a not unsightly pink by the sun). A white towel hangs from the arm of the chair and on the floorboards is a ceramic mug. He finishes the page he is writing and looks up expectantly, as if he has been waiting for your arrival. And he has such eyes! Blue-green and frightening in their clarity, they are the eyes of one standing at the shore, staring across a sun-bright sea. He returns to his tablet.

Don't look so frightened.

The boy goes closer and says something to him. The man continues writing, paying him no attention.

You came from the tight-fisted earth, and now look where you are.

"La Tondeña?"

I can't let you stay here, Kasa–

"Rum La Tondeña?"

— but I'll offer you a better conclusion than the one history does.

The boy claps his hands to get attention. He is getting impatient. "Rum La–?"

"Yes!" I boom. The boy jumps back, his small torso quivering with quick breath. "Yes, you little gamin," relenting finally. "I'll need it once I'm finished. And some San Miguel. San Miguel. Four," showing him on my fingers.

"Mango?" he asks hesitantly.

I extend him a lump of paper from my pocket. "No, I told you before I don't want any mangoes." He steps forward for the money. Steps back again. He counts it very carefully, then folds it and shoves it deep into his pocket. He looks at me inquiringly. It is double the usual. He is doubly suspicious. "Yes, the rest is yours. Go on then," I prompt him. "I have something to finish."

To Otomo Yakamochi

If it were death to love,
I should have died for you —
Just once.

One writes a letter

One writes a letter, taking particular care to see that all aspects of it are in accordance with one another; one adorns and embellishes it with all the imagination one is capable of, to prove to the addressee that one has depths which may never have been percieved; then one waits for the answer. It is vexing if the reply does not arrive soon. One tells oneself at every moment that it cannot be much longer before something comes. By the time that dog rounds the corner, the telephone will ring. By the time that ship rounds the point, the mailman will come. But these ploys are ineffective. The answer does not come and one is no more assured than otherwise.

It is always best to reply promptly to a letter, no matter what the answer.

I sold my robes for passage

I sold my robes for passage to Etchu at an inn on the outskirts of Naniwa. The owner of the house was very much surprised to find a lady of the Court at his front door and immediately ushered me into a dark corridor. He took a burning taper from the floor and led me to a small courtyard where the eaves impinged upon the light and the sky overhead was reduced to a doubtful square. There I explained to him what I wanted. Once the arrangement had been made — one robe for each day of travel (after that I could only guess at the fare)

— he told me to take a seat upon an empty saké barrel and wait for him. When he returned he carried what looked like a great deal of sacking over one arm. This sacking, it turned out, was a collection of the crudest clothing imaginable: square, baggy pieces of hemp that were to be thrown or tied over various parts of my body in a kind of patchwork. It was with extreme reluctance that I took leave of my comfortable silks, pleasantly scented with jasmine and a days' perspiration, to dress myself in those scratchy folds. When the man turned around to see me, he bellowed with laughter.

I complained bitterly that Otomo would not recognise me, much less want to in such rags.

"Well if he doesn't know you, neither will anyone else," he argued. "That's the whole point. You're the driver's wife for the next two weeks."

So begins my journey to Etchu. Each day we set out by first light, cross deltas, climb valleys, meander through foothills, wind among mountains until coming to some pre-destined place for the night. The driver and two grooms seem to know the route well, for there are days that we travel only for several hours before stopping at a village. The next day is, invariably, long and painful. Even so, we are sometimes forced to bivouac in open country, 'grass for pillow.'

In my life at Nara, I could never have imagined it, but I actually enjoy these nights spent in the wilderness. The driver, afraid of bears, sleeps on the roof of the carriage no matter how cold it is, while the grooms build a fire and sleep nearby. They hope that I will be content to remain inside the carriage on such nights, but I prefer to pull out the last of my good robes, concealed beneath the seat, and take a place near the fire with them. At first, this upsets the two grooms. They grumble about being unable to sleep with a 'plum' nearby.

But I am stubborn and they are usually too exhausted to put up much resistance to my wishes.

I would think at such times

I would think at such times of Koto and the life of a maiden at Isé Shrine, its stern rituals morning and evening, the long hours of inattention in between, and the empty renown that comes with that life. I pitied her. Boredom, when there are men around, is a sort of indulgence, a lull between bouts, more often than not filled with anger, annoyance, or anticipation. With nothing but nuns and monks around and few of the pleasures of the Court, Koto's life at Isé had to be very dull indeed. I decided that I did not envy her. Though I was uncomfortable, cold, hungry, and exhausted by travel — though no one could possibly choose my present circumstances over the pampered life of Isé — I could not help but feel that I was luckier than she.

Though every

Though every hill, valley, forest, clearing, or copse has its own startling panorama to reveal or conceal, each its own charming, garden-like arrangement of foliage and stone and water and shade, the days of a long journey become uniform by repetition and one begins to wonder if everything is being repeated over and over, the carriage and one's brain going around in circles.

Sometimes I am horrified by the speed with which routine consumes the world. Like a man on a voyage, I have found that every island paradise soon looks the same. Perhaps better eyes than mine, a better mind than mine, could distinguish subtler differences? This is a thought which is most infuriating. One wants to leap up and scream out loud to throw off the insidious, oppressive balance of the day.... Calm down. Are you crazy? Whatever are you hoping to prove? Better to dull with a bit of saké the twinge of one's own insulting ignorance than pantomime for blind gods.

The night of the Festival of the Great Bear

The night of the Festival of the Great Bear and Deity of the North Star, the young Prince Asaka went missing. In the uproar ensuing all the destruction that had been done at the Saké Bureau, his absence went unnoticed until late afternoon the next day when his nurses realised that no one was keeping watch over him. A casual search was mounted but the boy was not found. As the afternoon wore on, the news began to spread around the palace, and I could see a look of concern upon people's faces. It was then that I was called to see the Chamberlain Fujiwara, so I did not learn what became of the Prince Asaka.

There is hope

There is hope that we shall soon arrive. During a meal at what I had thought was a remote mountain temple, a monk with whom we were eating — I had long since given up my courtly manners and would sit down to eat meals with the driver and the grooms — mentioned casually that he was going down to the sea at Etchu on horseback the next morning to pick up some fresh shark.

I stared at him in astonishment. "Etchu?" I mouthed. There was no response. The driver and the grooms went on pushing dirty handfuls of rice into their sunburned faces. "Etchu?" I tried again.

The driver looked up at me. "Yes, Etchu. That *is* where you wanted to go, isn't it?" The grooms found this very funny. "You mean *that's* where you wanted to go? I thought you wanted to go to Edo!" They carried on the joke at great length, taking turns informing the others of the places to which they thought they had been travelling — Nara, Dazaifu, China, Persia. Their ability to parlay one simple question into an evening's entertainment was incredibly tiresome. Still, the monk eventually agreed to convey a note to Governor Yakamochi for me, announcing the arrival of 'a poet'. I went back to the room I had been given and tried to go to sleep.

When morning came I was in a great state of agitation. No sooner had we started out than I was retching out the side panel, rejecting everything superfluous to my state of excitement, quivering violently as a zither string.

The scenery which appeared in my small window was identical to that of yesterday and, frustrated by the lack of variation, no sign whatsoever that we were nearing the coast, I closed the panels and sat back in the seat, trying to deny to myself what I had heard the night before, lest the men had all been playing a cruel joke upon me. Several hours into the day I was lulled to sleep by the constant creaking and swaying.

When I came to, I leapt forward to the shutter. The carriage was winding down a hill. We were still in the forest, but through the trees I could see chalk-white streaks of surf far below. Now the coastline would slide around and a ridge of pines shift into its place, now the ridge would slope to the right and reveal the coastline again. When finally we stopped turning back upon ourselves we passed from the thick forest of cedars to one of pines and sandy ground. The carriage rattled less across the softer soil and I could smell the sea in the breeze.

Early in the afternoon we emerged from the trees onto a wide, white beach beneath a rent sky. Sunlight and shadow flooded across the sands in turns. We made straight for the water, the ox labouring across the soft sand. The driver yelled at the two grooms and they jumped down to push the carriage from behind. My four walls swayed from side to side as if we were on the sea until we came down the gentle slope to the water and the sand held firm beneath the wheels again. Bright glassy waves crumpled and frothed only yards away. Swiftly the wide arc of a wave advanced from the tumble of the surf and rushed beneath my vantage, splashing over the wheels. The grooms cried out happily and the ox moaned with fright, straining in its pole harness.

A tiny yellow flutter like a flame, moving quickly, caught my eye. Far down the beach, I made out a tiny horse and a rider carrying a tall banner. When he rounded the curve of the bay I could no longer see him from the side window. How I wished I was in Lord Hirotsugu's carriage, the one with the hole in the roof! I would have put my head out and waved to him. Here I am! I've come so far! Panting with anticipation, I pressed my forehead against the palm weave of the carriage wall, straining to see forward through a tiny hole.

A rocky headland arrayed with pines fronted an army of torn clouds fleeing inland from the sea. Nearer at hand, the horseman was advancing along the beach. Soon he was close enough that I could see his yellow banner clearly, the characters written upon it rippling fast in the wind as if under running water. He was arrayed in ceremonial grey dress, and the mantle of bronze upon his horse was resplendent beneath the intermittent sun. But I could not keep my eye focused upon him. The whole beach and sky and sea were suddenly awash in my emotions. The ox groaned loudly. Another wave had come to shore and, spreading wide across the sand, filled the last remaining distance between us.

ACKNOWLEDGEMENTS

The author would like to thank Patricia Hubert, Richard Perkins, Catherine Bush, Marcel DeCoste, David Widgington, Kirk Johnson, Meg Sircom, English 674, Steve Luxton, Gerald Luxton, Andy Brown, and — above all — Robert Allen for their enthusiasm, incisiveness, and vision.

Several books assisted greatly in the research for *The Pillow Book of Lady Kasa*. In order of importance, they are:

The Historic City of Nara: An Archaeological Approach by Tsuboi Kiyotari and Tanaka Migaku, UNESCO, Paris; The Centre for East Asian Cultural Studies, Tokyo, 1990.

The Pillow Book of Sei Shonagon, translated and edited by Ivan Morris, Penguin Books, New York, 1986.

A Collection of 10,000 Leaves, edited by Theodore DeBary, Columbia University Press, New York, 1965.

The World of the Shining Prince: Court Life in Ancient Japan, Ivan Morris, Kodansha America, New York, 1994.

The Pillow-Book of Sei Shonagon, Arthur Waley, George Allen and Unwin Ltd., London, 1979.

What is Japanese Architecture? by Nishi Kazuo and Hozumi Kazuo (Contributor), Kodansha, Tokyo, 1985.

The author and publishers are most grateful to UNESCO and The Centre for East Asian Cultural Studies for permission to reproduce images from *The Historic City of Nara: An Archaeological Approach* by Tsuboi Kiyotari and Tanaka Migaku, UNESCO, Paris; CEACS, Tokyo, 1990.

An image of Nara from *What is Japanese Architecture?* by Nishi Kazuo and Hozumi Kazuo (contributor), Kodansha, Tokyo, 1985 appears in Figure 5 without permission from the publisher.

The photograph in Figure 15 is courtesy of Mr. Scott Hayter.

The illustration of the Great Supreme Hall in Figure 11 was drawn by Ozawa Hisashi.

The aerial illustration of Nara in Figure 5 was drawn by Hozumi Kazuo.

Most of the poems in the text are drawn from the DeBary translation of *Man'yo shu* ('A Collection of 10,000 Leaves'), the great compilation of Nara Period poetry.